TWISTED LOVE

BILLIONAIRE BULLY DARK ROMANCE

SUMMER COOPER

Lovy Books Ltd
20-22 Wenlock Road
London N1 7GU

ALSO BY SUMMER COOPER

Read Summer's sexiest and most popular romance books.

DARK DESIRES SERIES
Dark Desire
Dark Rules
Dark Secret
Dark Time
Dark Truth

An Amazon Top 100
A sexy romantic comedy
Somebody To Love

An Amazon Top 100
A 5-book billionaire romance box set

Filthy Rich
Summer's other box sets include:
Too Much To Love
Down Right Dirty

Mafia's Obsession
A hot mafia romance series
Mafia's Dirty Secret
Mafia's Fake Bride
Mafia's Final Play

Screaming Demons
An MC romance series full of suspense
Rough Start
Rough Ride
Rough Choice
Rough Patch
Rough Return
Rough Road
Rough Trip
Rough Night
Rough Love

Check out Summer's entire collection at
www.summercooper.com/books

Happy reading,
Summer Cooper
xoxo

Keily

"*I* hate you, Keily. I don't know why I'm fucking you."

The way he'd groaned those words a month ago still played in Keily's mind like a song that she just couldn't get out of her head. Not that she wanted to, not at all. They were the most sensual words she'd ever heard in her life and still thrilled some secret part of her that she hadn't known existed.

He'd owned her in that moment, every single part of her, but she'd never tell him that. You didn't tell a man like Logan Sinclair that you liked him. You smiled at him, flirted, fucked him, sure--at every possible moment--but you did *not* tell him you liked him.

She wasn't that kind anyway, not anymore.

Maybe she never really had been, she decided as she looked in the mirror on the back of her closet door. The dress was suitable for the evening, black lace over nude silk that fitted her curves perfectly and came down to her knees, with lace sleeves that trailed down to a point on her hand. It was a vintage dress, far too expensive for her, even when she was married to Joe. It was a dress that Logan paid for. Much like the long, black wool coat she'd put over it when she walked to the door.

With a faint smile creasing the corners of her lips, she applied lipstick, dabbed at a black spot of mascara that was deposited near the edge of her right eye, and noted the gray eyeshadow perfectly matched her eyes. Nice.

A spritz of the perfume Logan had ordered for her and she was ready. A slim hand smoothed the French twist that turned her hair into a silky sheet of gold as she left the bedroom of her apartment. The apartment Logan had decided she could stay in, even though she didn't work for him anymore. At least not in the office. But definitely in the bedroom.

Her phone buzzed on the coffee table in the living room and she raced to pick it up. It would only be Logan, or Rosa perhaps. She and the other woman hadn't stopped being friends when Keily quit her job and Rosa still came over and called as often as she used to.

Violet still didn't call her and never sent text messages. That part of her life still stung, and she didn't realize how much she'd come to love her niece until she stopped seeing the adorable little girl. Maybe she'd go and try to see Violet this weekend. If Logan didn't take up all her time.

Are you going out with Logan tonight? Rosa's text asked.

That smile twitched at the corner of her lips again as she saw the words. Rosa knew everything that was going on, how she'd quit her job, the fact that she and Logan were sleeping together, and that Logan had basically made her his trophy wife. He paid all of her bills, gave her an allowance, and had allowed her to keep the company car. The apartment he'd provided her became their love-nest and he spent more time with her than at his own home. They did go back to his place sometimes, but not often.

She swiped a few buttons and Rosa soon answered.

"I take it you are going out, then?" Rosa chuckled knowingly.

The call instead of a text reply gave her away. "Yes, we are."

"Where are you going tonight?" Rosa sighed with good-natured envy.

For a moment, Keily wondered if there was a way to get Logan to invite Rosa along too, she was

Keily's friend after all. Maybe that dinner they were supposed to go to next week. Keily made a mental note to ask Logan about it and finally answered her friend. "To that Greek place. He's meeting with some buyers and I'm needed to smile pretty and make the other men there jealous."

"That is a job," Rosa laughed before she continued, "and you could make any man envious of Logan. You're beautiful, but you know that."

"Well, I did win all those beauty pageants when I was a kid, but I'm not sure I'd win as many anymore." Keily sighed, thinking of all those years she wasted on those pageants, and Joe.

"I'm sure you would. I'm going to get to bed early then and watch some Netflix. I hope you have a good evening."

"Thanks, Rosa, I'll call you tomorrow." She hung up the phone once Rosa said her own goodbye and walked out to the door. She'd just heard Logan pull up.

She looked down at the shoes she had on, the ones that Logan still had a thing for, and hoped that the other pair she'd ordered as a backup came soon. These were starting to look a little worn. But they would, since he insisted that she put them on so often. That brought the smile back to her face while she threw her coat on. She picked up a delicate bag that carried only a compact, her lipstick, her phone, and a small wallet with some money and her ID in it. The bag was barely big enough to hold her phone, but the black lace and silk matched her dress, so she'd chosen it for the evening. The chain was so thin it was almost an illusion, but it held up as she put the bag over her shoulder.

Logan had a scowl on his face as she walked out the door, but it soon turned into a smile when she got into the car. "Hi."

"Hi back. You ready to go?" He asked as she buckled in, his brown eyes watching her until she'd snapped the buckle in.

"Yes, you can go now." She liked the fact that he waited until he knew she was secure in her seat before he ever moved the car. A small thing, but important.

"How was your day?" He asked absently, his head moving around as he backed out of the spot in front of her apartment.

"Fine, same as usual." She looked out of her window as the other apartments passed her by, her thoughts on what the night would bring. "How was yours?"

"Well, the grandmother the temp agency sent me as your replacement broke her hip last night, so I went to visit her in the hospital and then went back to the office to find out who they'd sent to replace her. Rosa said she might have someone permanent instead, which would be a good thing."

He could be an utter asshole sometimes, but he could surprise her and be utterly sweet too.

"That's kind of you." She looked back at him, noted the strong jawline and how his hair now covered his ears. "You need a haircut. It's getting long."

"I thought you'd like it that way." He turned his face just enough to wink at her before turning it back to the road.

"I do, actually." She said thoughtfully. She did like the boyish look it gave him. A sudden need to touch him took over and she leaned over to place her hand intimately high on his leg. "I really do."

The words were whispered into his ear seductively, as a mistress would, but Keily didn't think of herself that way. She was his partner. Not his girlfriend, not really a trophy wife even, though she felt like one. She was part of the reason men found him charismatic and easy to deal with. They envied Logan the woman that accompanied him, and that brought more money to the company because they wanted a little bit of the success he had.

They hadn't talked about what they were, but it wasn't necessary. Not to her. She knew what she was, and it wasn't a mistress. Mistresses were kept out of the light, hidden away, not displayed and part of a strategy. Although, if she was honest with herself, they'd never talked about a strategy for these dinner meetings either. They were usually too busy getting each other naked when they were alone to talk about anything.

"You know I don't like it when you try to play while I'm driving, Keily." He brushed her hand away but stroked her cheek with the same hand before he put it back on the wheel. "Accidents do happen."

"Sorry." She muttered but she wasn't. It was all part of the tease, the runup to what would happen later when they walked in through her apartment door.

"It's alright." He turned the radio on then, putting an end to the conversation.

Just before they pulled up to the restaurant Logan turned the radio down.

"I've been thinking we need a nice warm vacation somewhere. Have you been to Hawaii?"

"Yes, I have." She answered quickly but didn't fill him in on the fact that it was a prize she'd won in one of those beauty pageants back when she was in high school, working the pageants for all she was worth.

Her mom had started her off in them on a whim when Keily was a baby and continued when she figured out that she could sell the prizes Keily won or turn them into cash. That had fueled a drug addiction that Keily still didn't want to admit her mother had. It was another reason her parents moved away; her dad hoped a change of scenery would help her mom get clean. So far, it hadn't worked. Keily still had no clue what happened to most of the prizes and had a feeling she'd never know. Explaining anything about the pageants might lead her to reveal too much though, so she kept it simple and sweet.

"I see." Logan shook his head and smiled at her before he pulled into the parking lot. "Well, think of something. If we need our passports let me know."

"Sure." She answered, kind of pleased that he wanted to take her away on a vacation. She needed to get through this dinner before she could think about vacations, though. She checked herself in the mirror on the back of her visor and then got out of the car. Logan pulled his overcoat out of the car and put it on before he headed over to her.

They walked into the restaurant together, their hands linked. Logan gave his name to the woman at the hostess stand blocking their entrance into the restaurant. Keily noticed the way the woman's eyes ate Logan up and how she smiled as if she'd seen the most delicious thing on the planet. The woman very well might have, but he was Keily's. At least for now.

She had no illusions that he would keep her around forever. She hoped he would, but Logan was the kind of man that didn't make promises he couldn't keep. After the woman seated them at a large round table, Keily sat down next to Logan. Four other chairs ringed the table but she wanted to be by his side. That was her role now.

The waiter came and they ordered their drinks. Logan asked the waiter to hold the menus until their guests arrived. A few minutes later three men and a woman came in and were brought to their table. Two of the men were in their thirties, full of cocky self-assuredness. The one in a tailored black suit with a shimmery silver cotton shirt looked Keily over before he looked at Logan with a speculative look.

Keily knew what he was thinking, it had happened before. Was Keily part of the deal? Logan's lips tightened and his stare turned steely. The man's eyes went up for a second but then he smiled. "Logan, great to see you again."

"Nice to see you too, Allen. How's the wife?" Logan asked the man with black hair styled to within an inch of its life. The man opened the buttons of his suit jacket before he sat down as did the man in a gray suit beside him.

"She's great, Logan, thanks. I haven't been here before, have you Bill?" Allen asked the other young man.

Keily looked at the man in the gray suit, noted his blond hair was cut professionally but lacked the layers of styling products that Allen's sported. He also wore a wedding band, and he didn't look at

Keily like a hungry wolf. She smiled politely as the man named Bill nodded.

"Yes, I've brought Lisa here before. Logan, this is my wife, Lisa, and I guess you know Shane." Bill held his hand in the direction of the older man, around fifty, Keily guessed and smiled up at them all.

Lisa sat down beside Keily, a friendly smile on her face. Kiely liked her taste in fashion, the red Armani fitted dress showcased Lisa assets perfectly. She also liked Lisa's smile and calmness. "Hi, I'm Keily."

"Nice to meet you, Keily." The woman with black hair and dark brown eyes put out her hand for Keily to shake.

Yes, she seemed like she'd be a good companion for the evening. If only Logan wasn't so distracting.

"What are you having?" Lisa asked as she looked around the restaurant.

"I think I'll have the steak. It's hard to go wrong with a steak." Keily answered. She'd need the energy for the hours later when Logan would show her just how high he could make her climb.

She glanced over at him as Lisa went quiet while she studied the menu. He was as handsome as ever, smiling confidently at Shane as they discussed something Keily couldn't hear. Logan laughed, a real laugh, not one of those fake ones he usually gave clients. He liked Shane then.

The waiter came to take their orders and they relaxed together as they waited. A bottle of wine was brought to the table and Keily poured it expertly. Logan watched with approval, his eyes on her hands as she held the bottle. She knew what he was thinking about from the way his nostrils flared: Her hands wrapped around his neck as she rode him into oblivion. She caught his eyes when he glanced up and her cheeks went pink. Yes, she'd need that steak and maybe dessert too.

Logan caught Lisa's attention when he started to tell a story about one of his company's products: a self-defense device, and how it had saved someone's life. Keily's thoughts drifted, she knew the story, and she thought about that vacation he'd mentioned he wanted to take her on. He'd suggested Hawaii but she'd been there before.

Maybe one of the islands, or somewhere cold where they could cuddle in front of a fire. It was a hard decision when a man offered to take you wherever you wanted to go. She'd ask him to take her to Europe, but everybody went to Europe when they got the chance. Where could she go in America? she wondered. Alaska maybe, with wild secluded nights in the woods.

In the end, though, she knew it wouldn't matter. Wherever she went with Logan, she would end up in his arms. She loved this life he'd given to her, and she planned on keeping it. She'd destroy anyone that tried to change that.

"Another glass of wine?" Lisa asked and distracted her from her thoughts. The pretty woman wiggled the bottle left and right, her eyebrows raised in question.

"Sure, let's drink to a good night and happy lives." Keily took the glass of red wine with a smile that reached all the way to her gray eyes. "To us."

Everyone else raised their glass to join the toast and Keily's smile grew wider. She had them all under her spell, just as she always did. Life couldn't get any better.

2

Logan

*H*e'd fuck her out of his system one way or another, he reminded himself as he drove into work the next morning. He'd spent over two hours last night wrapped in her arms, with her legs wrapped around his head, with his arms wrapped around her. It hadn't been enough but soon, he knew he'd get his fill of her. He always grew tired of women.

Logan drove into the parking lot and locked the car as he exited. He'd made it to his office and was just sitting down in his chair when Rosa, Keily's BFF and the head of his HR department, walked in with a happy smile on her face.

"Keily's replacement will be here soon." She

leaned against the door jamb, her brown eyes and dark hair a picture in the early morning sunshine.

Logan didn't feel even a smidgen of attraction although he should. Rosa was a gorgeous woman but all his body, all his brain craved, was Keily. The women of the world might as well all be men now for all he noticed.

"That's great news," Logan left his office and headed into the outer office, where his PA would work. There was a coffee machine that was calling his name. "Coffee?"

"No thanks, I have some back at my desk, I just thought I'd let you know the woman should be here soon. We're early." Rosa lifted her chin to the clock on the wall and he noted that it was almost 7 am. She wouldn't be late for another half an hour.

A ding of the elevator made them both turn to look at the doors as they slid open. A woman in her late fifties with steel gray hair and a no-nonsense face walked out. Her lips were coated in a pink, matte-finish lipstick but that was all the makeup she wore. Her hard brown eyes stared at Logan as she left the elevator and walked into the room. The swish of her light-pink satiny quilted coat created a soundtrack for her steps as she came to stand in front of him.

"Mr. Sinclair?" She asked, her large hand out to reach his. She must be six feet tall, he thought as he stared up at the old-fashioned bun on top of her head that must have added another three inches to her height.

"Yes, you must be my new PA. I'm sorry, I wasn't given your name." He looked at her quizzically and she smiled, a real smile this time.

"Monica Williams, Mr. Sinclair." She clasped his hand as he put out and shook. "Nice to meet you."

"Great, thanks for coming in, Monica. Let me show you around." Logan nodded at Rosa who left the office after a brief hello to Monica. "Let's get you started, shall we? This is your office, that's your desk…"

Logan tried not to drone on but there was a lot he had to say to Monica. Her pay package wasn't as big as Keily's had been, but it was generous. Monica also had a home and a car of her own, so he didn't have to provide those things to her either.

This wasn't turning out so bad, after all. He could get work done because he wasn't distracted by Keily, worrying about a potential lawsuit from Keily, or the many and varied ways he wanted to fuck her in his office. Monica was married, had grandchildren, and was already showing promise. She'd been laid off from another business that folded and was grateful to Logan for the job.

"I know it must not be easy for a company to hire a woman of my age." She said as he hovered in his doorway, ready to get to work now that she had arrived.

"I never really understood that Monica. Older people bring knowledge and experience with them. At the end of the day, a young person can become just as sick as an older person, so I don't see the problem." He smiled a genuine smile but not one of his thousand-watt smiles. That might have blown her away.

"I'm glad you see it that way, Logan. I'll look over the folder that has the instructions in it and get started."

"Thanks, Monica." Logan nodded and closed his door at last.

He'd taken out some of the instructions, they were things he'd added in there simply because he knew Keily had lied on her resume. He'd wanted to make her hate him, instead, she ended up on her knees for him. And her back. And her front. So many different positions.

He smiled as he took his seat and wondered if he'd think about her all day again. He wasn't after love with Keily, in no way was he looking for that, but he did find her fascinating. She was curmudgeonly, biting, downright mean when she wanted to be, but she could also be very gentle, kind, and full of laughter with others. One of his favorite memories of her was of her laughing with her head thrown back.

He got to work but an hour later Monica knocked on his door. "Delivery, sir."

"Thanks, Monica." He took the brown package from her and opened it once she'd left his office. It was the platinum diamond and sapphire necklace he'd ordered for Keily from a jeweler in California. A delicious creation that would wrap around her neck beautifully.

She absolutely purred when he bought her gifts, and he knew this one would be a triumph. She'd adore this as she had all of his gifts so far. He'd bought her clothes, gifts for the house, and a lot of shoes. He'd spent hours scrolling through websites looking for the perfect heels for her. Always stilettos, always high enough to make her calf muscles pop, and always sexy. She had quite a collection now because of him.

A ping from his laptop and phone made him remember where he was, and Logan put his thoughts of Keily away. He was only having fun with her, that's all, and he had to stop wasting so much time thinking about her. She'd be gone soon enough, and he'd have his life back.

After he got her out of his system.

He was even careful not to give their relationship a name. When he introduced her to anyone, he introduced her as his date. She wasn't his girlfriend or anything else, she was just his date. The woman he fucked every chance he got.

Monica thankfully interrupted his thoughts to ask about the coffeemaker and how it worked.

Normally, he was busy by the mid-afternoon. but it was a quiet day today, and everything was going well in all his buildings. Even the California branch was slow today.

Around lunchtime, he went out for a meeting with the local bank. He wanted to set up an account there, bring some more money into the local economy. That went quickly, and before long, he was back at the office wondering what to do with himself. He knew what he wanted to do, but he was trying to control himself today. He'd have to back off from her soon enough, or she'd overtake his every waking moment. She was even in his dreams, although he didn't want to admit it. He told himself he couldn't remember the things he dreamed about, but he did.

Logan pondered it all quietly because he didn't have anyone else to talk to. He'd been alone most of his life, and he'd never had a best friend. Keily was actually the closest thing he'd ever had to one. She didn't know all of his secrets, not nearly all of them. If she did, she'd probably run, but he'd let a few things slip out.

He was just so relaxed when he was with her, even if he knew that could be, would be, a mistake. If he allowed her to get too close, he'd be really fucked up. He reached for his computer, hoping for an email and message he needed to answer. Instead, he found himself looking at the vacation rentals he'd been looking at last week.

A chance to get away sounded nice, even if he'd still have to do a little work while he was gone. Which was another reason Monica had shown up when she did. She'd have to handle a lot of the calls he'd get while he was away. He looked at a website for a cabin in Colorado. A nice winter scene was set in the pictures, a romantic getaway in the woods.

She'd probably want somewhere tropical though, with hot nights and gentle breezes. That's what everybody wanted, wasn't it? He frowned, knowing he'd take the snow any day of the week. He loved winter and hated the heat and sweat that came with the summer months.

He hated it even more when he started wearing suits daily. It was a lot of clothing to wear just to look professional. He'd wanted to fit in though, so he'd replaced his carpenter shorts and t-shirts with Armani suits and got a haircut. He'd been surprised at how much his appearance changed and noted how the suits brought confidence to his stance. He liked the change and hadn't gone back to his old look.

Now, if only he could get Keily out of his system so effectively.

Another knock and he called out for the person to come in.

"Hi, it's me," Rosa said as she came into the office and closed the door. "I'd like to have Keily over for dinner one night this week, you too if you want to come, and wondered when she'd be free? She said she isn't sure, so I thought I'd ask you."

Rosa's tanned cheeks turned a bright red, and her eyes were glued to the floor. She was embarrassed and Logan felt bad about that. Keily was his target in this game he was playing, not his staff.

"Oh, um, well, tomorrow night would be good. And I'd like to join you, but I'll have to see if I'm free or not." He kept his eyes on her and when she glanced up, he tried to make her feel less embarrassed. He was fucking her former colleague and best friend, not committing a crime. Okay, so he'd kind of set that woman up as his literal mistress, and he paid all her expenses, but that wasn't a crime, was it?

"Great, let me know and I'll make enough for us all." Rosa quickly ducked out of the office and Logan made a note to find some acceptable gift for her.

He spent the rest of the day playing a game he'd found online. Last week, he'd have taken off early if it was this quiet, to spend the time between Keily's luscious thighs. He'd decided to slow things down a little though, make sure she knew he was the one in charge and that she had everything she wanted because of him.

His gaze flicked to the box the necklace nestled in. Maybe she didn't realize it, but every gift he bought her was a decoration for her, his pet. The same way some women dressed up their toy-sized dogs, he was dressing up the woman he fucked. Which was brutal, but it was the truth.

He didn't want to admit that it was him that needed the reminder. Keily wasn't what he'd expected, she had learned her job well, so well he'd hated to lose her, but loved her new position, so to speak. She'd been an asset to his team by the time she'd quit and had made his life easier for him.

But she'd quit, in no uncertain terms. With those words, she'd set him free to do exactly what he'd wanted to do for an exceedingly long time and that was kiss her before he fucked her senseless.

Now, he couldn't stop thinking about her, even when he kept reminding himself to. Like now.

Frustrated he got up and left the office. Monica had already figured out what calls to forward to him and which to take messages on, so she simply gave a wave when he walked out of his office and said he was leaving for the day.

It was an hour until his normal quitting time anyway. Well, those nights when he left the office before midnight. Some nights he'd stay even later but lately, things had run smoothly for him. Which was good because he was way too distracted with the woman in his life.

He got in his car and drove out of town, not towards Keily's. He headed out to the highway and just drove in a random direction. It didn't matter where he went because all he wanted to do was listen to music and drive his car. Traffic wasn't bad yet and he managed to get on the interstate easily. He could be in Florida in less than half a day if he ignored the speed limit. He could even stop somewhere in Georgia, maybe Savannah or Atlanta.

The idea didn't appeal to him, though, not without Keily at his side. He needed a break from his own thoughts but even out here he couldn't. He'd never admit she was anything more than a fling, but he wondered, for a second, if this was another lie, he told himself.

Keily wasn't the kind of woman you threw away, even if she was a former cheerleader and had married her high school sweetheart. A sweetheart that she'd eventually had the sense to divorce. That must have really hurt her pride, to admit to all her friends around here that Joe wasn't the guy she'd painted him as.

He knew women like Keily, or the Keily he thought she was. The kind that had beautiful houses, beautiful bodies, and worked hard to maintain that image. Appearance was everything, and he wondered how hard it was for her to keep their relationship quiet. But, then again, he knew she was a lot different from the woman he'd thought she'd be.

She wasn't really that woman at all. Sure, superficially she was. But he'd seen her in an old suit on the day she walked into his office, full of pride and determination. That must have stung, too, wearing that old suit to a job interview. But she'd done it with confidence and the poise taught to her at an early age. He'd learned a little about her, knew about her background in beauty pageants, knew she hated the things now.

He turned around, headed back to her place with the present on the seat beside him. He was learning too much about her, he thought. It was time to stop talking so much and start fucking more. Before it was too late.

3

Keily

"So, you hired the older lady?" Keily spoke out loud, her phone resting on the kitchen counter picked up her voice. She could hear the sound of fingers tapping against a keyboard from the phone's speaker.

"Yes, but not just because of you, honey," Rosa's voice came from the phone and Keily nodded at her friend's answer.

She laughed softly, wishing she could have seen Logan's reaction to his new PA. With practiced fingers she gathered up celery to chop on the chopping board for the chicken soup she was making.

"I know, but still, thanks." She kept her eyes on her fingers as she chopped the celery. "It's good to know he won't be distracted at least."

"It's not like even the prettiest of the applicants would have been any kind of competition for you, Keily." Rosa mused and the typing paused. "Logan barely even looks at any women when he actually comes out of his inner sanctum."

"I've noticed that." Keily hummed and paused in her chopping. "Still, it's nice that there will be someone competent in the office for him."

"As long as she isn't sexy, beautiful, or even remotely interested in Logan, right?" Rosa laughed and went back to typing.

"It's that interested in Logan part that's most important. Interest creates problems, even if the man isn't looking at the other woman." Keily had looked away often enough when she was married to Joe, and he'd caused quite a few problems for them both. She'd always found that the women that were interested in him, but he didn't look twice at, caused more problems than even he managed to create.

"Tell me about it," Rosa muttered and Keily knew the woman had stuck a pen in her mouth, something she often did at work when she was doing too much at once.

"Take that pen out of your mouth, Rosa, you'll ruin your jaw clenching it on that pen."

"It's better than smoking," Rosa complained back at her and Keily had to agree. "Anyway, if I get off the phone, I can concentrate on this. My lunch break is almost over so I'd better go."

"You'd better, and don't forget to open your office door back up." Keily chuckled to herself as she said it. Rosa often forgot to open the door again if she stayed in for lunch and people would walk right by it thinking she was out. How they didn't know by now that a closed door meant nothing where Rosa was concerned, was beyond Keily.

Rosa went back to work and Keily went back to preparing dinner. She almost had the soup and bread ready with a smile on her face by the time she heard Logan's car pull up outside her apartment. He didn't knock before he came in, just waltzed in like he owned the place. Technically, he was the one paying her rent, so she didn't complain. Besides, it was nice to know he felt that much at home with her.

"Hi." She murmured, walking up to him with a wide smile. "How was your day?"

She slid into his arms, admiring his caged strength when his arms wrapped around her gently. It felt good to be so close to him, to smell his cologne, and to just...feel him. She let her head sink to the place beneath his right shoulder that held her head so perfectly.

"It was good, dinner smells nice." His finger came up to brush at her hair, loose around her shoulders, before he planted a kiss on the top of her head and pulled away.

"It's chicken soup with French bread I made this afternoon." She answered his unasked question. "It was all I could think of to make."

"Sounds good. I'm going to shower and then we can eat." He waited for her to nod before he walked away.

He'd taken off his suit jacket and wore only a dark gray button-up shirt and his black slacks. Those slacks did wonderful things for his ass and she enjoyed every second of watching him walk away. She loved to watch how his muscles moved, revealed themselves, as he walked away, and knew she'd get to explore all of those lovely places on him later. He'd had a present in his hand when he walked in so tonight would be a good night.

Keily's lips quirked up into a pleased smile as she walked back into the kitchen and poured the homemade soup into two bowls and cut up the bread. He often brought her these little gifts; expensive treats that made her eyes light up. Every now and then words she didn't like to think about, ugly words that questioned her character popped into her head, but she knew that wasn't what this was. Logan was just…kind.

Dinner was on the table by the time he came out, a thick black terrycloth towel wrapped around his waist. Her eyes went wide as he waltzed into the room, chest still sprinkled with water. The broad plains of muscle that banded his chest flowed down to the hills and valleys of his abs, where a line of water traced down below his belly button to draw her eyes to a path that was stopped by the place where he'd hooked the towel together. Her mouth watered as she remembered what was hidden beneath that towel.

"It looks great," Logan said, coming up to her to kiss her cheek before he went to a chair and sat down.

Disappointment drew her eyebrows down for a moment before she smoothed them out and went to her own chair across from him. She smoothed the black material of her long-sleeved t-shirt dress down over her lap and picked up her spoon. "Is it warm enough for you in here?"

"Yes, it's fine." He looked up at her, heat burning in his eyes. He picked up his spoon instead of leaving his seat, so she picked up her own as well.

He wanted to wait to get to the fun stuff. Well, that was fine with her.

His eyes drifted down to the deep V of her neckline in a way that told her he wasn't as immune to her presence as he pretended. Desire made his nostrils flare, but he didn't put that damned spoon down.

Truth be told, she didn't care what kind of gift he'd brought her tonight, he'd brought her so many she was becoming a little bored with them. Well, not really bored, since he brought her such nice gifts, but something about them had started to unsettle her a little. Perhaps it was those words she kept at bay in her mind, nagging at her.

She didn't care if Logan never gave her another gift, all she wanted right now was him. Deep down, she'd started to like the way she felt around him. She felt safe, adored, wanted, all of which were things she'd never really felt before. As a child, her mother wanted to use her for pageant prizes, her husband wanted a housemaid and a body to find pleasure in. Even her sister needed her as a babysitter more than she did a family member.

"Are you alright, Keily?" He asked, his attention fully on the soup. "This is good by the way."

"Thanks, and yes, I'm fine." She put her spoon down in the bowl and looked over at him. "Why?"

"Well, it's just that your cheeks are a little flushed."

"Oh, yes, I'm fine. It's just a little warm in here, that's all." She hedged and looked away. It was all a part of the game. Tempt him, tease him, and then she'd get exactly what she wanted from him and it wasn't whatever was in that box.

"I see." He continued to eat, the short sentence all the answer she knew she'd get. He'd talk when he felt like it.

She tasted her soup, found it delicious as

always, but didn't really notice. All she wanted to taste was that spot between his neck and his clavicle. That silky spot, that was only one of many, but one of her favorites.

"Do you want more wine?" She asked a few minutes later when she noticed his glass was almost empty.

"Yes, thank you." He sat back in his chair and she watched him as she stood up, his gaze on her feet.

She'd figured out he had a thing about her wearing heels and had deliberately slipped them on after she sat down to eat. All part of the plan.

His left eyebrow lifted a little, but he didn't speak. His eyes didn't move either, they just became a darker brown and narrowed at the corners with interest. She moved up next to him, her left knee pressed against his thigh. Instead of moving the wine glass closer, Keily leaned over the table, knowing the hem of her dress would ride up…just enough to reveal the white expanse of her plain cotton panties.

She immediately felt his hot palm on the expanse of her upper thigh in a soft but possessive clench. If only those fingers would move a little bit higher. Logan wouldn't do that though, he liked to play, he liked to take his time, and she loved every second of it. She looked back at him, smiled, but said nothing. She poured the wine to the appropriate level and then stood up. "Anything else?"

"Ahem, no." He moved his hand away and picked up his spoon again.

Taking her seat once again, Keily picked up her spoon and went back to her own dinner. The bread was dry and tasteless in her mouth, though she knew it was just as delicious as the soup. Nothing would taste good, nothing would bring her pleasure, not with Logan in the room. Only he held her senses, and only he could give her pleasure.

"Perhaps you should take off your dress if you're hot." He broke the silence in the room.

Her breath caught in her chest. He was ready then. She brought her face up to look at him. "Perhaps. I'm not that hot though."

Not yet, were the words she left unspoken.

Aware that his eyes were on her, she pulled her legs up into the chair, letting one shoe dangle from her foot. Let him come to her, she decided. Even if all she wanted to do was crawl to him.

Logan picked up his napkin, wiped his mouth, and let his eyes meet hers with a defiant air that was tinged with awareness. Two could play that game, his gaze said.

Her lips twitched up at the corners, a smile of victory that wasn't quite dazzling yet.

"Are you finished eating?" He asked as he stood

up, not admitting defeat at all as he gathered his dishes.

"I am." She answered and watched him take the dishes away before she picked up the glass of wine, took a gulp, then put it back down.

"I brought you this." She heard him say as he came back to the table, a box in his hands.

"Oh, it's lovely." She responded as expected, and held the necklace up to him so he could put it on her. "It's beautiful, Logan, thank you."

"Not as lovely as you." His fingers brushed against her skin as he brought the edges of the necklace together to clasp it behind her neck. He must have felt the shudder of anticipation that wound down through her body as liquid heat at even that slight touch, but he said nothing.

Cold stones and metal rested against her skin in a display of sapphire and diamonds that dazzled him if the look on his face meant anything. She was burning for him already. It wouldn't take long for the cold metal and stones to warm up, not with the heat her skin was throwing off now.

She slid down from the chair, ready to thank him properly for the gift he'd bestowed on her, to selfishly take what she wanted from him, which was the real gift. Every moment of pleasure she gave to Logan was the best gift he could give her, even if he didn't know that. She wanted to feel the silky but hard length of him between her lips, on her tongue. She wanted to inhale his scent while she swallowed him down her throat to the sound of the groans he couldn't hold back, no matter how hard he might try.

The mere thought of giving Logan an oral thank you was an intense experience for Keily, a fantasy she often played with. Some men seemed to think that a woman sucking their dick put her in some kind of submissive position, and some women saw it the same way, and it could be if you didn't take control. And Keily took control every opportunity she had with Logan. She loved having him in her hands, loved making him lose all control.

That was a completely different kind of pleasure, one that made her desire unbearable but something she endured with wicked glee. He'd see to it that she got her own relief from that torturous pleasure, one way or another.

"Stand up, Keily." Logan rasped out when her fingers brushed against the zipper of his black slacks. "I want a different kind of thank you tonight."

"Oh?" Her eyes went wide, and her eyebrows lifted in question. He'd decided to stay in control then. The hint of a smile that played at the corners of her lips was met with a smug smile.

"What?" He asked, his voice low and almost a purr.

"Nothing, I just thought you might like…" she let the words trail off and held out her hand as she stood up.

"No, my dear, not tonight." He shook his head to add to the no. "Tonight, I want to hear you purr for me."

"As you wish." She lifted her chin slightly, met his gaze, and stared back boldly. There was nothing timid about her tonight. She wanted to push his buttons, to get a response from him, and she'd do it with defiance if that's what it took.

4

Logan

*L*ogan knew what she wanted the minute she slid down to the floor on her pretty knees. She wanted to blow his mind, and him, but that wasn't what he wanted tonight. He knew she loved having him at her mercy, but tonight she'd be at his. That's the thank you he wanted. That's how he wanted it. That's how he'd have it.

"Back against the wall, please." He told her, his fingers trailing along the back of the chair she'd pushed back.

The smirk she threw over her shoulder was naughty, one that invited a nice swat on the bottom, but he'd let it go for now. He knew she'd end up in a delighted puddle at his feet if he gave her the spanking she wanted. He'd found out she loved the slaps against her firm ass during that first week they'd spent together but used it sparingly, as a treat and nothing more. He did enjoy the squeals and mewls of delight they produced though.

Tonight, he wanted to bring her to heel, to show her who was in charge and that it was most definitely him. Not her. "Take your dress off."

She moved to pull the dress over her head revealing the firm tone of her body, a body that needed little exercise to stay just how he liked it. Not that any input from him would make her workout more, or less, she did as she pleased and he hated to admit it sometimes, but he liked that fact. Her body was hers, as it should be.

"No, leave the shoes on." He instructed quickly when she made to step out of them. She did that on purpose, he just knew it. He frowned at her, but inside he was smiling. She knew how to play him.

"That's it, leave them on." His voice was little more than a whisper, but she heard him. He knew she had, even if she didn't respond, because she stood back up straight against the wall for his inspection.

She took his breath away, leaving him to stand there staring at her in amazement. Normally, he would have been disappointed in a pair of plain cotton panties but the way the fabric hugged her hips and cradled her sweet pussy was just as sensual as any lace or silk panties could ever be. She didn't hide her full breasts or pretend to be shy by looking away. Instead, she met his gaze directly until he looked down at her shoes. Those shoes did things to him, things he didn't understand, but he didn't care.

He had a feeling that direct gaze was still on him, but he was as unashamed as she was. He wanted her to know she was desired, that he wanted her, even if his brain told him he should be backing up, packing up, and heading back to California and far away from her. He was losing ground with himself, with the inner battle between the man who'd overcome all the odds and the boy that had only ever wanted to matter, to have a woman like Keily look at him just like she was looking at him now.

Finally, when she shifted slightly, he moved. Slowly, he walked up to her in the dim light she preferred in the dining room and traced his fingers up the left side of her waist. Smooth silky skin met his fingertips and he looked down at her. Even with the heels she still had to look up at him and that tinged his smile with perhaps a little too much superiority.

"Stay there, Keily. Don't move unless I tell you to." His voice rumbled enough to make her shiver, he noted, and that smile grew broader. Or maybe it was the words? She always wanted to be in control, to be the leader, but when he demanded she give in to him she became a kitten, ready to play.

"Yes, Logan." She answered him, her face defiant, but he knew it was all part of the game. She'd scratch his back to shreds later, partly because she'd lost control, but mainly because she'd want to make sure he knew she'd been there. Every little scratch would be a reminder the next day, one he had to admit he liked too much.

"Stand still." His fingers traced up her ribs to the full expanse of her right breast. His fingers gently stroked the delicate skin beneath the globe before they trailed up to tightly grip her nipple, a move she hadn't expected. She'd expected gentle, appeasing, but not tonight.

Tonight, she'd get one surprise after the other.

He applied more pressure to the tender flesh, and she hissed, but it wasn't in protest. The moan that came after the hiss told him that. Her back arched, pushing her breasts higher into the air, and he couldn't refuse the invitation. He kept his fingers on her right nipple as his teeth clamped around the left one.

"Logan." She gasped his name as if the word had been spoken without her notice and he knew it probably had. She loved having her nipples teased and the harder the better. Not always, but most of the time, Keily was a woman that thrived on having her nipples teased mercilessly.

With his free hand against her stomach, Logan continued to tease her, but the bite turned to suckling as his fingers moved lower. Her breaths came tighter, closer together, as the hand slid down to the very edge of her panties. That breath caught in her throat when he stopped moving his hand and sucked harder on her nipple.

"Please, Logan." Keily's plea was followed by movement from her hips, only a slight hitch, but enough to draw his attention.

He was as hard as a rock, ready to plunge into her, but he waited. He could handle himself, he could handle the pain, because he knew he'd be deep inside her soon enough. When she'd come apart all over his face.

"What do you want, Keily? Tell me." He demanded but she only shook her head against the wall, so he took back the nipple he'd allowed to pop out of his mouth.

"Fuck you, Logan." She panted, but didn't say anything more.

His only reply was to brush his fingertips against her abdomen, just above her panties, until she shuddered against him. She took it as the warning it was, play along or you don't get what you want. He smiled against her breast when she whimpered a sound that he knew was her acceptance. She'd still argue with him, one way or another, but she'd answer his demands now.

"I want to come, Logan, don't make me wait." The words came out in pants and he knew she hated the weakness she couldn't fight. She wanted him, just as he wanted her, and neither one of them could help it. Or stop it, it would seem.

"All you had to do was ask." He said hotly against her breast.

He immediately knelt down in front of her, pushed her feet apart, and kissed her abdomen. He allowed the edge of his fingers to tug only slightly at the bottom hem of her panties, near the warmest part of her, as he brushed another kiss below her belly button. "You are so delicious, baby."

"Just shut up and get your face in there, Logan." She answered with a growl of her own and he smirked at the feral quality of her voice.

"Now, now, kitten, don't get in too much of a hurry because I mean to take my time and make sure this is done right." He answered with a chuckle before he hooked his thumb into the top of the cotton material and tugged it down.

She moved to let him slide the panties off before she settled back against the wall, still in the heels. Her feet were planted apart, enough room for him to explore as he pleased, and explore he would. With his hands clasped around her outer thighs, he moved closer to her. So slowly he could barely stand it himself, he moved towards the dewy lips of her opening. They folded beautifully over the hidden flower inside, inviting his lips to part the folds.

He kissed the edge of the slit that separated her folds before he pushed his tongue into it, to taste her fragrant, delicious taste against his tongue. It was a heady taste, a taste he'd never forget and wanted to taste a million more times. He moaned against her as his tongue became saturated with her flavor, his head buzzing with pleasure. When he found the tiny hill that was her clit, he flattened his tongue out until she groaned and buried her fingers in his hair.

That was the spot, the place where he could so easily become lost in the wet heat of her desire, but he'd found it and would stay honed in on it until she sank to the floor. His desire to prolong her torture was forgotten the second her fingers tugged at his hair and her ass tilted to give him better access.

Logan worked his tongue on her, in tight circles that would get her off fast and hard. He was eager to get inside her but that wasn't what drove him. The need to hear her gasp as she came was a wild force that took his control, that made him act to quickly make her come. His fingers clutched tightly, almost bruising her thighs, something else she liked, and he'd give her whatever she wanted as long as it brought him what he needed. If she wanted that hint, that thrill of pain, he'd give it to her.

He loved the sensation of her silky thighs against his cheeks, the heady scent of her right there in his face, easily lapped up onto his tongue. Everything about this woman turned him on and he lost himself when he was so intimately close to her. And when he heard her responses, the way she gasped or panted at his touch, it nearly made him lose his mind.

But he had to get her off first. That was his mission.

"That's so good, Logan." She groaned. She was close then, he knew it.

Her hips jerked in time with his tongue as he slowly tongued her clit, then sucked her. Hard.

Her legs began to quiver, and her hips thrust against his face sporadically. With his strong fingers buried in the fleshy globes of her ass, Logan held her there on his lips as he sucked harder.

"Logan, fuck, Logan, please, I'm so close." The woman of his dreams begged.

He moved a finger on her ass until he found the spot that would send her over the edge. He could thrust his finger into her there, but he knew the tease of it was what she wanted. Oh, she'd get off if he slid his finger into her ass, but the tease of not doing that made her nearly scream with pleasure.

A quick glance up showed him tight nipples,

ready for his tongue, a mouth open as her body tensed around his face, ready for his cock. She responded to his slightest touch, be it his breath, or his mouth, his fingers, or his cock, and she loved having him touching, inside, every inch of her. Oh yes, he'd had, and would have, every part of her, but he knew, deep down that, it would never be enough.

She was like a drug he wanted to quit but couldn't. He'd started this as a game, as a way to regain some of the pride he'd lost as a kid, but it had become something he couldn't control, not always. He was a grown man, he knew that, and knew that his pride had been salvaged a long time ago, but the minute he'd seen Keily's application on his desk he knew he had to have her, to make her the one that paid for all the pain and humiliation he'd endured back when he was a geeky kid without a friend.

Now, he seemed to be the one paying the price, but it was a price he loved paying. Her essence flooded his mouth as she came apart above him, her body now a writhing snake but he held on, he drove her higher until she groaned loudly, in capitulation.

He held on as wave after wave of pleasure made her body dance in sensual abandon. He wanted to film it so he could watch her at his leisure, to see every emotion that crossed her face.

She probably wouldn't agree so he hadn't bothered to ask her.

When her body went limp and she tugged at his hair he leaned back and looked up at her. "Done?"

"You're going to kill me one of these days. My head's just going to blow right off." She sank down to the floor, her eyes on his, full of sated happiness.

"I'm not sure how I'd explain that to the authorities." He answered and pulled at her hand until she stood back up. "We aren't done."

"Mm, you're determined to find out what you'd say to them then, aren't you?" She leaned into him, her lips hovering just below his. Her heavy-lidded eyes looked into his, full of filthy promises he knew she could keep.

"I might be, but right now, all I'm interested in is getting inside of you." He guided her back to the table. She marched in front of him on unsteady legs until her thighs met the edge of the table. "Lean over."

He thought she'd give some witty rebuttal. Instead, she leaned over until her hips were at just the right angle, the heels still on her beautiful feet. He loved the curves of her body, the way her full hips pinched in to form her waist. He clasped his left hand around her waist as he guided his cock to her entrance, the black towel he'd had tucked around his waist was long forgotten on the floor.

He wasn't thinking anymore, only feeling. What

he felt most was desire, a need to feel the way her walls clung to him, sucked him in. He needed the way he lost his own mind when he was deep inside of her and she made all those lovely sounds he loved so much. She moaned when he sank into her, a sound of encouragement and delight. He gave an answering groan, clenched his other hand around the other side of her waist, and jerked her hips back to his.

"Like that, Logan, just like that." She demanded, and he answered, pounding into her as he jerked her hips back onto him over and over again.

Logan lost all control, her every word, sound, and movement a goad to lose himself in her. So he did just that. She started to pulse around him, her walls fluttering around his shaft to stroke every drop of his pleasure from his body. He groaned her name as he came apart, totally lost in the only woman he should have never touched.

5

Keily

"I don't care what anybody says, having hair pulled out by the roots anywhere fucking sucks." Keily waited to hear Rosa's response over the speaker system, turning right out of the beauty salon's parking lot to head home.

"Girl, don't I know it. At least you're blonde and have fine hair. Try having coarse dark hair." Rosa said softly. She was still at work, but even with her office door closed there were some things she wouldn't say too loudly.

"I can't believe we pay to have that shit done." Keily was swearing like a sailor but didn't care. The waxing experience had been extra painful today for some reason and she didn't like it to begin with. "Needs must, I guess."

"I guess. At least you have a man that will appreciate your efforts." Rosa sighed on the other end of the line, her loneliness obvious.

"I'm sorry. I guess I shouldn't complain." Keily really meant it and wished she could find somebody for her one and only best friend.

"No, honey, complain away. I forget sometimes I shouldn't make people feel bad by laying out my own misery in that way. We all have problems, complaints, and I shouldn't belittle yours."

Keily smiled even though Rosa couldn't see it. Rosa really was that good a friend and Keily appreciated her thoughtfulness. "You're awesome, do you know that?"

"I do, but men don't seem to notice. Maybe I should try with the other team or something?" There was a laugh in Rosa's voice, but there was something nervous about the laugh that caught Keily's attention.

"Um, is there someone you have in mind?" Keily was curious and wanted to know whatever secret it was that Rosa was hiding.

"Maybe, we'll see. For now, I'm only going to say that I'm considering a few things."

"I see." Keily's smile only grew bigger. Rosa *was* talking to someone, Keily just knew it. "You'll tell me when you're ready, I guess."

"I will, you know I will." Rosa sighed again, a

sound Keily was awfully familiar with lately since she'd done so much of her own.

"My sister still won't take my calls." Keily all but whispered. "I guess I deserve it."

"From what you've told me, yeah, maybe. But you're a different person now." Rosa paused, not sugar-coating anything, whether Keily was her best friend or not. "She'll come around one day. I know she will."

"I hope you're right. Listen, traffic's getting a little heavy now, I'll call you back later, alright?" Keily's finger hovered over the 'end call' button as she waited for Rosa's reply.

"Of course, deal with the traffic first. How about I call you when I get off work?"

"Sounds great, honey, bye for now," Keily said, glaring at the button now.

"Bye, Keily. Be careful."

"I will," Keily answered and hung up. "Now, are you going to make up your mind about which lane you want to be in?"

Keily's glare turned from the button on the screen to the black sedan swerving in and out of the lane. The driver was lucky there wasn't anyone coming in the other lane because they'd have caused an accident if there had been.

It took Keily ten more nerve-wracking minutes to get home, the black sedan swerving across every lane before they turned off at the apartment complex just before Keily's. She'd have called the police, but she was afraid to take her eyes off the road long enough to call 911. At least the idiot driver had made it home. Now, whether they were drunk, tired, or having some kind of medical emergency, they were off the road at least.

It was the most exciting part of Keily's day, that swerving driver. The waxing had been the most painful, but not exciting. The haircut she'd also had at the salon was nice, but it wasn't that exciting since it was just a trim. She'd even had her nails done, a red and black ombre that she loved, but…it wasn't really exciting either. The whole package was more to kill time than to make sure she was presentable to Logan. She had extraordinarily little to do now that she was a, ahem, kept woman.

As she went through her front door a thought occurred to her. She hadn't checked on that scholarship business in a while. Logan's mention of a vacation a while back had made her brain kick in. She'd won scholarships in those pageants on top of all the other prizes, were they still available? She'd emailed a few places about the scholarships she'd won, but then she'd forgotten about them. Maybe they'd gotten back to her?

Keily changed into a slouchy red long-sleeved t-shirt dress, put on some red fluffy socks, and walked back into the kitchen. With a press of a button, her laptop came to life and she sat down at the kitchen table, one foot on the chair as she opened her email. There were a few replies, all of them automated messages telling her someone would contact her soon, but nothing else.

Turning her phone over, Keily swiped until she heard the line ringing and Rosa picked up the phone.

"I thought I was calling you back later?" Rosa chuckled and Keily smiled.

"Yeah, you were, but you remember me telling you about that scholarship money I might have?"

"Yeah. Have you heard back from them?" There was a note of excitement in Rosa's voice and that made Keily's smile turn into a frown. Even Rosa would be disappointed with her news.

"Just an automated message. But I need help."

"You know I'll be glad to."

"It's been a while since I've even thought about those scholarships. If my mom didn't find a way to turn them into cash, I might have enough money to get into a good university with an online program. I asked my mother about my prizes more than once, but she always said I lost the prizes for one infraction or another."

"Infraction?" Rosa sounded as doubtful as Keily felt.

"We could lose the prizes if we broke anything in the contract we signed with the pageant runners.

Getting caught drunk, which I did a few times, or things like that."

"Were you arrested? Can they really take prizes away?" Rosa asked with obvious doubt.

"Mom said they could. I saw things like that the few times I had enough time to actually skim the contracts. Mom always rushed me about signing them."

"I see." Rosa paused, spoke to someone on her end of the line, then spoke again. "What do you need me to do?"

"I did a little snooping back before I graduated high school and found out what happened to most of the prizes. A drawer in mom's bedroom revealed everything in bills of sale, printouts of transfers, and a savings account in my name that she kept hidden from me." Keily paused, memories of that drawer were a little overwhelming. While the truth had rocked Keily's brain, the little bag of crystal meth and the pipe her mom used to smoke it with nearly broke her heart.

That bag had explained a lot to Keily, and it wasn't just the fact that her mother had gone from beauty queen material herself to a woman who looked twenty years older than she was. The drug ruined her mother's skin and teeth, but the worst part was how it had made her personality and thinking change. The clear shards of the meth had become so important to her mother that she stole from her own daughter and that hurt Keily the most. The truth had changed who she was that early spring night and for a long time, Keily was a hard, cold person. A person she hadn't liked, at all. A person that Keily didn't exactly want to discuss even with Rosa.

"That's awful, Keily. What kind of mother does that?" Rosa gasped and whispered with shock.

"Mine." Keily said morosely.

The horrible things her mother had done were a major factor in why Keily had made a change in her behavior, in her thinking. Yeah, she was still looking out for herself, but she wasn't that girl who'd turned away when others had needed her most, well, not since she'd started working for Logan. Which was why she was hoping her mother hadn't been able to do anything with the scholarship money. The cash prizes were all gone, the balance on the savings account had told her that, but what about everything else?

"I was thinking. I have to wait for an answer, but I've looked at a few of the 'for-profit' schools, and the research I've done on them showed that some are good schools, but most are scams. I've moved my search to in-state universities and found that the state university offers several online programs and mixed-mediums classes. Those are the ones that sometimes offer online and sometimes in-person classes. I've looked through them and found a few programs I liked."

She'd gone through their enrollment checklists and knew she'd have to call her old high school to find out about getting copies of her SAT scores and everything else. It wouldn't be hard to do and she'd added the call to a to-do list she'd started. Also on the list was a box for checking her emails more often and calling if she hadn't heard back from any of the places before the weekend.

"Okay?" Rosa drew the word out, clearly not sure where Keily was going with this.

"Sorry, I'm being vague. I need help deciding on what to major in."

"Oh, that. Well, what do you like to do?"

"I really liked working with Logan. And not just because I wanted him as more than a boss." Keily laughed. "I liked the job."

"Then focus on that. Or whatever you like. I'd suggest doing an aptitude test, or something like that. Those are helpful I hear."

"That's a good idea." Keily nodded, even though Rosa couldn't see her. "I'll let you get back to work and do that."

"Thanks, honey. I have a meeting I need to get to, so I'll talk to you later, okay?"

"Sure, have a good afternoon."

Keily hung up the phone and looked up the test Rosa suggested. There were hundreds, but Keily decided on a free one. She was frustrated when she got to the end and had to insert her email address to get the results but did it anyway. She was curious.

The results arrived quickly, and she was surprised at the answers. There were suggestions that she'd never considered, but she did see administrative assistant down near the bottom of the list. She had a few options to think about then. With all of that done, Keily headed into the kitchen to start Logan's dinner. The hell she'd paid a pretty penny to put herself through earlier made her more than a little uncomfortable, so she decided to get something delivered instead. Everything in the fridge and freezer would require her to move around a lot and stand up longer than she felt comfortable with at the moment, so the delivery option was the one she took.

Logan wouldn't mind, she knew. He didn't mind it when she had food delivered because she always chose the best places to order from. Life wasn't so bad when he was so easily pleased most of the time.

Logan was good like that, and even if he didn't want to define their relationship, even if she knew this might not last forever, she enjoyed the time she did get to spend with him. Lately, her emotions had been on a rollercoaster and she vacillated between wanting to make sure she wrung every last drop of enjoyment she could out of her time with him and making sure she walked away with as much as she could.

That was the old Keily rearing her ugly head though, the greedy cow in her. She'd had quite a lot stolen from her at a young age and that had really made an impact on her ever since. People would screw you over, even your own mother, so it was best to screw them first. But that was an ugly way to be and she didn't want to be that way anymore, not really.

Logan had kind of made it clear that was what she should do though. Every time he called her his 'date' or didn't define who she was at all, it hurt a little and the old Keily would come back into play. The need to put that Keily to bed was another reason she wanted to go back to school. She'd had plans when she went off with Joe to help him get through his university days. He'd taken those plans from her. Another hurt on the list of hurts she'd collected over the years.

Being a victim wasn't a part of her plans anymore, however. She still hated what her mother and Joe had done to her, what she'd allowed Joe to do to her, but she knew she had to pick herself up, brush off the dirt they'd thrown at her, and get on with her life. Nobody was going to come and save her.

Except Logan, a little tiny voice in her brain

tried to whisper. She squashed it. Logan wanted to fuck her, and he would until he grew bored with her. Then he'd throw her away too. The minute she stopped being what he wanted her to be or someone more interesting came along, he'd dump her on her ass.

Getting an education, a degree, would be a good idea. She would be able to stand on her own two feet and, yeah, it might just be a piece of paper, but the work, the study, the research, and the knowledge she'd gain wouldn't be useless. It would hopefully open doors for her. She went back to her computer and started doing more research into which degrees were the most profitable. She didn't necessarily want to go into a medical field, so she scrolled past those and looked at the other listings.

Nothing really interested her or caught her attention. She thought about the things she liked to do and knew singing wasn't something you could really profit from, not without a huge fanbase. Besides, she hadn't sung in front of an audience since her high school days.

She'd really liked working for Logan though. Maybe that was the right field to look into since she kept going back to it. There was time to think about it, and she didn't even know if she had the money to afford the classes yet. There were student loans and grants, but she wanted to avoid anything she might have to pay back later. Going back to school was about making a clean slate, about starting over, and having debt hanging around her neck before she even finished a degree wasn't the way she wanted to go.

The jewels and other presents Logan gave her would certainly pay for more than a few semesters if she sold them, but he might ask for those back once he was done with her. She didn't have the money to fight him on it if he did demand the gifts back, so she didn't enter them into the equation of what her future might be.

Thinking about the future wasn't so depressing now but still, as she settled on the couch in the living room, Keily realized she'd be even lonelier than she was now. She missed her niece's baby laugh and giggles, she even missed her sister's frowns and the spats they'd had about Keily leaving a yogurt carton on the kitchen counter, something she didn't do anymore.

Violet wouldn't believe her sister had not only learned to clean up after herself, but to clean the house without a maid to do it for her. She'd told Violet all the things that had happened in her life, through emails and text messages, but there was never any response.

Tears formed and spilled out of Keily's eyes at the thought of her sister and Alice, the cutest niece an aunt could ever hope for. Luckily, Violet had been totally against entering Alice into pageants, which had set their mom off, even though she lived so far away now. Keily had been proud of Violet's adamant denial that she would ever do that to her daughter, even if the part about 'look how Keily turned out' had stung her to the core.

Keily had to admit, Violet was right. Those pageants had done a number on her and her mother. Her mom had admitted more than once that the meth habit started with the pageants. One of the other moms used it to stay awake and had offered some to the harried mother she'd found in tears. She couldn't kick the habit, even now when it was about to kill her. The woman was still using it, but tried to tell her family she had it under control and flat-out refused to go to rehab.

As for Keily, the pageants turned her into a snob, she had to admit. When she found out about her mom's theft, well, she'd come to see the whole pageant life as an ugly stain on her own life. If it hadn't been for those pageants, none of this would have happened and life might have been different. She might be a normal human being.

With a deep breath, Keily pulled a blanket over her lap, opened a book, and tried to put those thoughts away. It was time to look to the future, not the past. And now, if she had some scholarship money left, she even had a backup plan.

6

<hr />

Logan

"Do I really have to go?" Logan spoke in the car on his way to Keily's a week after he'd handed her his last gift. He'd had to work really late the last few days; a new product was launching, and he'd had to be at the office to oversee everything. This was his first chance to spend some time with her and he'd been looking forward to it.

Then he got the call that ruined his evening.

"Yes, it'll probably just be continued, but you have to be there if you want the judge to take this seriously. It's only assault and battery in the third degree, which would get him thirty days in jail with a fine if he wasn't on probation already, so I'm pushing for the judge to take it seriously. I can go alone, but it looks better if you're there."

"Fine, I'll be there." Logan groaned, noting the date a few weeks away in his calendar.

"Great, Logan, thanks. I've been wanting to nail this jerk ever since we were in high school." Felix, his lawyer, laughed. "I'd almost do this case for free."

"I thought the prosecuting attorney didn't charge plaintiffs anyway?" Logan laughed and shook his head.

"Yeah, you're right. I need to go back to being a defense lawyer, my kid needs a new retainer. How she keeps breaking them I'll never know."

"Kids find ways, you know that." Logan didn't know personally, but he'd been a kid once. Shit happened.

"Yep. Right, that's all I need, you be safe driving home."

"I will. I guess you heard the traffic?"

"Yeah, you could have rolled your windows up, you know?" Felix groused, but Logan just rolled his eyes. The prosecuting attorney was a good guy and had been a year behind Joe, Keily's ex, in high school, apparently. The man detested Joe and had made no bones about it. That made him a friend in Logan's book.

"I could have but then the noise wouldn't have

annoyed you, would it?" Logan quipped and heard Felix groan.

"You're such a dick, Logan," Felix said but laughed it off.

"I am. Talk later, Felix. Take care."

"You too." Logan heard Felix say just before he pushed the button on the display to end the call.

The call would only ruin the evening if he let it, he decided as he drove through evening traffic to Keily's apartment. He hadn't seen her in days now and he was eager to be with her. He couldn't believe it, but he missed talking to her, feeling her, even smelling her. His hands clenched on the steering wheel as he thought about her, his need for her growing.

He hated it, but he had to admit to himself that he wanted her. He insisted to himself that it wasn't getting out of hand, as he drove into a parking spot and turned the car off. He'd gone days without seeing her and it hadn't killed him. But he'd hated every moment of being without her. He squashed that thought with a frown and got out of the car.

"Hi there." She met him at the door with a smile, wearing only a long-sleeved t-shirt that barely covered her ass, much less anything else.

"Mm, hi there." He swept her into a hug that soon turned into a kiss as he pressed her against the wall and kicked the door shut.

He pulled away when he inhaled and scented

something delicious that wasn't her. "What's for dinner?"

"Well, I wasn't sure if you were coming but I made a Belgian stew and some bread to go with it." She replied and pulled further out of his arms. He noticed she was barefoot and frowned for a moment.

She was an excellent cook, that wasn't why he frowned at all. The stew sounded, and smelled delicious, it would taste the same way, he was certain. No, it was her lack of shoes that bothered him.

She was a great conversationalist and they'd had many conversations that intrigued him, made him think. And she was always eager for his touch, most of the time. The lack of shoes was a signal though.

He'd become accustomed to the subtle signal of her footwear since he'd become her lover. She'd always worn some very sexy shoes. He'd never realized he had a thing about women's shoes until he'd seen her in his office in those black heels. Those heels meant she wanted sex rough and dirty, usually as soon as he walked in the door. She wore boots when she wanted sensual and long play with him, a slow tease that lasted throughout the evening. But on evenings when she was barefoot, she wasn't interested in sex at all. After a long absence, he'd expected the heels to be on her feet.

He looked up at her to see she was grinning.

"Noticed that have you?" She asked with an

even wider grin. "I didn't know that you were coming, or I'd have put on some proper clothes."

She kissed his cheek and turned away. "Come in the kitchen, I need to stir dinner."

He followed behind her after he pushed his own shoes off his feet and walked in to see her stirring the pot happily. She had some music playing softly in the background, and a glass of red wine sat on the counter by the stove.

She followed his eyes and tilted her head. Those gray eyes of hers caught his attention and he forgot what he'd been thinking about.

"Want a glass?" She asked softly, and he watched as she picked up the glass and took a sip.

Her lips were beautiful, and he wanted her, but if the lack of shoes had indeed been a signal then he wouldn't push. Pushing meant they were in a relationship and hinted at a need that he didn't want to admit to her. He'd leave her be, if she didn't make any moves, he decided. But damn if her lips pressed to that glass weren't tempting to kiss.

"What?" He asked, knowing she'd said something but uncertain what she meant.

"Wine? Want a glass?" Her left eyebrow tilted up telling him she was amused at his state of distraction.

"Sure, yeah, sounds good." He nodded, stuck his hands in his charcoal gray trousers, and frowned at the floor. He was like some lovesick schoolboy and he hated it.

"Sit down, I'll bring our glasses over to the table." She gestured towards the table with her chin and he followed her directions, still not happy with himself.

Still, he'd been with her longer than he'd been with any other woman. Maybe it was time to allow himself to feel...something. Or not, he immediately rebuked himself. He was not the settling down kind.

"I might have some scholarship money, you know? For school." She added when his brows knitted together.

"For getting a degree?" He asked, even though she'd said she had one.

"Yeah, uh, another one." She lied smoothly, and he smiled again. She still hadn't admitted she'd lied on her resume. He didn't care anymore.

"Good. Education is never wasted, after all." He offered and she nodded.

"That's what I was thinking." She said and came to sit at the table in the chair next to him. She slid his glass over to him and took a sip from her own. "I might need another option in life, one day, and I have free time now, so what better way to spend it?"

"Indeed." Logan nodded again, looking away from her with guilt eating at him. She hadn't asked for a guarantee or definition of their relationship, but it was there, between them for the first time. "I think that's a good idea."

"Thanks." She nodded and he could see her disappointment, though she did try to hide it. He ignored the tight sensation in his chest and tapped his fingers on his glass. "Any other news? It's been a few days since I saw you last."

"Not much really. You said you were busy, so I kept myself occupied trying to find out about these scholarships and everything."

"Well, you're a smart woman, Keily. If you want to go back to school, I think you'll do great at it." He believed it and wanted her to believe that as well. She was smart, it was one of the things he liked about her most.

"Thanks. I didn't do too bad in school, when I bothered to pay attention, that is. I wasn't the best student when I was in high school."

"People need a little maturity sometimes, be less influenced by...outside forces and teenage hormones to focus." He said but felt like it might sound judgmental. "I just mean..."

"It's okay, I was one of those boy-crazed morons that spent more time worrying about whether my boyfriend would like my outfit and hair than my grades. I'm not saying it was the brightest thing to do but, I guess, well, I got it into my head that the only way to succeed was to marry well, and so that's what I tried to do." She shrugged and then went on. "I can't blame anyone but myself for where I'd ended up when you hired me."

Her eyes were clear, without reproach of any kind, and full of acceptance of her own decisions. She wasn't proud of those decisions, but she was proud of who she was at that moment. Logan smiled, seeing that look on her face wasn't something he'd expected from her all those months ago.

"Speaking of, I have to go to court in a couple of days over your ex-husband's shenanigans. The prosecuting attorney says it will probably just be a continuance, but I have to go."

"Oh. Well, I was a witness, do I need to go too?" She turned to him, her face clear and open for once, a woman who truly only wanted to help.

"I don't think so." Logan shook his head and touched her cheek, cupped it, as he smiled down at her. "No need to drag you into it until it's totally necessary, right?"

"I don't mind. I don't know why I haven't been subpoenaed; you'd think the prosecutor would have done that already." She leaned into his touch, her eyes closed and Logan simply...enjoyed touching her.

"I'm sure he'll get around to it, don't worry." He moved away and let her have some room to breathe.

"Well, dinner will be ready shortly, if you want

to wash up or anything." She got up from the table abruptly, a knot between her eyebrows.

Something was bothering her, but he wouldn't push. Keily would talk if she wanted to. Trying to force anything out of her was like trying to force water out of a stone, he'd learned that long ago. She'd talk if she wanted to.

He had an idea of what was troubling her, though he didn't want to think about it any more than she wanted to talk about it. They'd been sleeping together for a while now; some might even call it a relationship. Even if it was one based on sex and nothing more. But was that all it really was? a little voice jabbed at him.

Of course, that's all it was, he knew that, even if getting up and walking away felt like he'd just let her down somehow. He went into the bedroom they shared when he stayed over and changed into some black cotton pajama pants and a t-shirt. He'd shower later, he decided, for now, something drove him to get back into the kitchen with her.

"That smells really good." He said as the scent of fresh bread and the stew melted into his nose once more.

"I'm glad you think so." She replied, something shy in her glance. She looked away quickly and put the lid back on the pot. "I'll get the bread out of the warmer and cut it up. Want to set the table?"

They worked around each other as he selected

tableware and she poured the stew into a serving bowl a few minutes later. She set the bread and the stew on the table and they both went quiet as they started to eat.

Logan watched Keily, uncertain of how to proceed. He didn't want to be in a relationship with her but staying over on a night when she'd worn no shoes meant he was there for more than sex. Was it a good idea to keep doing that? One look at her beautiful eyes and the way she smiled at him told him he wasn't leaving tonight for anything. Not even if that part of his brain that wanted to protect him from hurt told him he should run as far away as he could, as fast as he could. Before it was too late.

7

Logan

*L*ogan once again pulled into a parking spot at Keily's, ready to see the one woman he knew he should be avoiding. It had been a week since he'd pulled up to her place last, that night when she'd greeted him barefoot. He'd left the next morning and been called out to California to handle a supply issue. His team there couldn't handle it and he'd had to go.

Then he had to rush back to go to court with Felix. Joe had been there, looking as surly and unkempt as ever. Logan smiled the entire time he was at the courthouse, watching Joe's rage build as he stared back at Logan. It probably wasn't the smartest idea to continue to antagonize someone so unbalanced, but Joe deserved it for what he'd done to Keily, and to him, Logan reminded himself. He deserved so much more than a slap on the wrist, that was for sure.

The prosecutor had explained that since Joe was already on parole, this would probably get him sent to prison. Logan couldn't imagine being so wrapped up in self-pity that he ensured he'd end up in prison for the sake of beating up a guy that was dating a woman who'd left him.

But was it dating? He kept thinking of her as the woman he was fucking, but sometimes, stray thoughts slipped in. Words like 'girlfriend', 'relationship', and 'the future' crossed his mind and it was starting to become unsettling. That day in court, that had been worth the threat of further aggravation. But not prison.

She knew he was on his way, though, he'd made sure she knew that for a fact.

They'd exchanged texts all week, heated messages full of desire and need. Now, he was back at her place and he wanted her so much he was worried they might not get the door shut before he planted himself inside of her this time. His breath shook in his chest as he pulled the keys out of the ignition and pushed the door open.

He'd wanted to surprise her, show up unannounced, but it bothered him, the way he felt when he thought about her delighted surprise. He didn't surprise her, not because she'd enjoy it, but because he would. It was all very fucked up, as far as he was concerned, but it also made a strange kind of sense. To him.

He approached the door, lit by the porch light to chase away the darkness, knocked, and pushed it open when he heard her call out. She was walking to the door as he entered, a smile on her face but nothing else on. Well, nothing except those black heels.

Yes, he thought when he saw those shoes. He didn't have to take his time, he could take what he wanted, so long as he took her with him.

With a twisted grin designed to seduce, Keily walked up to him and slid straight into his arms. He couldn't help but capture her heated lips in an intense kiss as he wound his arms around her waist. When his hands grasped at her ass, she gave a little hop and wrapped her legs tightly around him.

Logan didn't hesitate to carry her to the couch where he laid her down long enough to take his clothes off before he joined her. He dug his right palm underneath her to slide down the long expanse of her silky back and purred when she arched at his touch. Her abdomen pressed into his as their eyes met.

He saw the all-consuming want he felt mirrored in her eyes and that rocked him in ways he really didn't want to examine, at all. Keily took over the moment when she reached for the proof of his desire, her bottom lip caught between her teeth, a dare replacing the want in her eyes. Let her have him those eyes dared, let her have what she wanted the most.

Logan almost stopped her but when her slim fingers wrapped around his hard length, he couldn't do anything but close his eyes and groan. Her cool fingers felt icy hot against his cock, but it was heaven to be in Keily's hand. Still, it wasn't as pleasurable as being inside of her would be. And if the way she tilted her hips up to him meant anything, he'd soon be inside of her.

"Keily…" He gasped her name as he felt the wet heat of her entrance against the very tip of him.

"What, Logan?" She teased with her voice before she tortured him by moving him to slide along her slit slowly before she pushed him back down. "Do you want something?"

"Stop teasing me." He insisted with a muffled grunt when she stopped at her opening.

"And do what, Logan? What do you want?"

"I want to fuck you, you little tease." He'd had enough and pushed against her hand, slid through her fingers, and straight into her welcoming slick walls.

She groaned as he plunged into her, her body opening just for him, only for him, he thought as he gripped her right hip to tilt her pelvis up to him. He wanted to be deeper, further inside of her, buried so far that he might as well have crawled inside of her and taken up residence. He wanted that soothing envelope of pleasure to embrace his entire body, which was about as poetic as he could be. Or was it pathetic? He didn't care he decided, as he began to stroke into her in deep, steady thrusts.

"That's it, Logan, just like that." The words panted out of her as he thrust into her, harder, then faster when her nails dug into his ass.

Logan flipped them over expertly before he pushed up onto his knees so that he could look down at her, his hands on her hips to hold her against him. He studied her, the deep red shade of her nipples, dark with desire, her cheeks flushed, her eyes burning gray orbs of fascination. Then there was the flat plane of her stomach, the flare of hips, and the place where their bodies were joined. He watched as his cock slid into her, fascinated with the gleam of her obvious desire coating him.

He nearly came then and there but curled his toes and met her eyes. "Not yet, baby. I'm not done yet. Come here."

He pulled out of her long enough to sit down on the couch properly and pulled her onto his lap. "I want those nipples in my mouth when you come."

She groaned happily, sinking onto him just as he took her right nipple in his mouth. His hands on her ass guided her to a fast pace that had her groaning his name in a way that made his balls ache for more.

"You're so soft, Keily, incredible." He said before he claimed her other nipple. "Now, make yourself come."

Her body went rigid for a fraction of a second, only a moment before she pushed her right hand between their bodies, eager to get off. She was so eager he grinned around the nipple before he sucked on it hard enough to make her wince, but it was a wince of pleasured pain. Just the way she liked it.

Logan distracted himself while he waited for that first fluttering sign that she was almost gone. Maybe she needed some help, he decided and let his fingers dig between the swells of her ass, to touch her in the most intimate way possible just as he bit down a little harder on her nipple.

That did it. He froze as the orgasm rocked through her, making her back arch and pull her nipple away. He followed along, held on, and sucked as her walls nearly swallowed his cock whole in gulping squeezes that nearly undid him.

When she'd started to climb down, when her nails no longer dug into his shoulders, he rocked up into her, held her hips still while he pounded himself inside of her with sharp thrusts that shook her. It was a reckless moment, one that he might regret later, mainly because he hadn't even put a condom on, but he didn't care. He wanted to be right where he was, balls deep in the only woman he couldn't seem to get out of his system.

"Keily…" Her name was a whisper on his lips as that first shot of his release made him seize up. He held her still with a tight grip as his body took over, his eyes somewhere in the back of his head as even his toes curled with pleasure. It was an intense moment, the slick feel of her against his naked cock was incredible, it always was though.

He felt the tension melt out of his spine as he sank further into the couch. Keily sagged against him and he wrapped his arms around her to hold her in place. He could go again, if she just held still for a minute. He wanted to fuck her again, wanted to take his time, renew his memory of her, even if his brain said he needed to run fast and hard away from her.

It was starting to become annoying, his brain's constant warnings to leave Keily behind. He hadn't meant for the affair to go on this long. He hadn't meant to melt at the sight of her gray eyes smiling up at him in satiated happiness. He hadn't meant to *feel* anything other than the pleasure of having her on his dick.

But now? Now he felt…something.

He nudged her to move and he got up, despite her groan of protest. "I need a drink."

"Oh, okay." She mumbled but he heard the hurt in her words.

He ignored the twinge of guilt that made his heart ache and walked into the kitchen to pour a glass of orange juice. He didn't want her to see the affection he felt for her, or the soft way she made him feel. Softness was for the weak and Logan was anything but soft. "I might go back to the house this evening."

"Oh?" She asked simply, a wall coming down over her face. "I thought you'd stay tonight?"

"I need to take care of some things over there, a water leak..." He let the lie trail off, unwilling to say more.

"I see." She pulled her bottom lip between her teeth and narrowed her eyes at him. When she let her lip go, she got up and walked over to him, just as nude as he was. "And you wonder why I hate you so much?"

She punctuated the question by grasping his cock, instantly hard in her hand. "I know why you hate me, Keily. I'm a bastard and I know it."

"Hmm." She nodded as she stroked him in just the right way, her grip not too tight and at just the right pace. "You are, but that's not why I hate you."

She looked right into his eyes, and he expected naked vulnerability, but she wasn't worked up enough for that yet. She wanted to be in control, to change his mind. He might just let her. "Why do you hate me then, Keily?"

"Because you make me hate you. Even when I want to like you, you make me...hate you."

"Then why are you stroking my dick?" He gave her a sardonic smile that made her blink before she answered.

"Because I love your dick." She whispered as she leaned up to his lips. Her tongue darted out, stroked his bottom lip, before she spoke again. "You've got a magic dick that's cast a spell on me, and I can't get enough of it."

"It's good to know." He rumbled with amusement. "At least you like something about me."

"That's about all, yes." Her lips quirked into a teasing smile, but he didn't really care if she meant it or not. He just wanted her to keep stroking his dick.

"That'll do." He murmured with his eyes closed, concentrating on the sensation of her delicate hand stroking him.

"Shall we move to the bedroom?" She purred into his left ear with a sultry whisper.

"No, the shower, I think."

"What about that water leak?" Sarcasm dripped from her every word, but she didn't let him go.

"Fuck it, it can wait. I need to fuck you again, then deal with that." He blinked to hide the look of conquest that raced over her features before she put it away. Fuck, he was in trouble.

She instantly pulled away and headed for the bathroom. He watched her hips sway, her feet still, somehow, in those heels. Fuck, he loved how they made her legs look. She paused at the door, turned just enough to wink at him, then headed in.

He was in so much trouble. He knew it but couldn't do anything about it.

Not when she was that close. That naked. That ready for him.

Logan followed her into the bathroom and found her already in the shower, her hair wet with shampoo rinsing down her back. His eyes found her wet breasts, traveled down to her flat stomach, and below, to the thighs that felt so good wrapped around his waist. Would he ever get enough of her?

Their eyes caught as he stepped in and she moved out of the stream of water. She turned him until he was the one under the hot spray, her eyes hungry to look at him. There was a black body scrubber in her hand, doused with the body soap he preferred, and she used it to wash him. All of him. By the time she put the scrubber back on the hook on the wall, he was ready to plunge into her.

Keily had other ideas.

She stepped out of the shower with a backward glance that dared him to follow and headed into the bedroom, wrapped in a thick black towel. By the time he dried off and made his own way into the bedroom she was on the bed, ready for him.

"I think I need a little attention, Logan." She let her hand stray down her body. Her legs opened, and he watched as her fingers slid into her folds. The middle finger of her left hand stopped on a spot he knew must be her clit because she began to circle the spot with sure strokes. "I need your tongue right here."

He loved the way she tasted, the way she pulled at his hair and lost control when he went down on her. "I'm happy to oblige."

He slid up the bed and settled between her legs. His hands under her ass guided her to tilt her hips up to meet his hungry tongue. He inhaled her clean scent just before he ran his tongue along her folds. She tasted like heaven and the moan that came from deep down inside of her was its own pleasure. Logan loved that sound.

He didn't take his mouth away from her as he put her legs over her shoulders and pulled her up, to get that sweet pussy of hers all in his face properly. She was soaking his tongue with her juices and he loved every bit of it. He'd go to sleep with her scent in his nose and it would be heaven. But not as heavenly as sucking her clit until she came apart.

Her thighs went tight around his head as he lashed at her with a relentless need to drive her over the edge, to hear those sounds that made his cock impossibly hard. He didn't have to wait long. That was another thing about Keily...when she wanted to come, she did. In quivering, clenching waves, she came apart and this time was no different. Her hips twisted, but she was trapped, riding his face while his tongue urged her to go higher.

Later, he'd fuck them both into oblivion. For now, he wanted to make her come again before she'd even come down from this one.

The 'leak' at his house was totally forgotten.

8

Logan

Are you coming for dinner tonight? The text Keily sent glared up at him.

Logan cringed with guilt and turned his phone over. He was in his office and it had been a week since he came back from California. He'd given her dozens of excuses, problems at the house, problems at work, problems in California, anything he could think of to keep her from getting upset. But that simple text carried a lot of meaning behind it.

Of course, she hadn't demanded to know anything more than if he was going to her place that night, but he knew there were probably more words there. Words such as, are you coming back, or are we done, words he didn't know the answer to. He'd left Keily's the morning after his return determined to put an end to the whole thing.

If he was a normal man, one that didn't have a hard time trusting others, he'd have a best friend to talk to. Sometimes, not often but sometimes, he wished he did have someone he could bounce his problems off, but he'd have to trust that person and there wasn't anyone he would trust with the thoughts he hid away.

A normal man wouldn't be running from Keily either. He'd be with her every second of the day that he could be. This week had been a test though. Not of her, of himself. He'd wanted to prove to himself that he could stay away, that he didn't need her. Even if he'd sweated out pounds he didn't need to lose on his treadmill every morning and night. Even if his dreams were filled with only her. Even if he found himself lost in daydreams, remembering the way she groaned when she came.

"Logan, will you be ordering lunch in today?" His PA asked from the doorway and he looked up to see the older woman there, a grandmotherly smile on her face.

"Pardon? Oh, lunch, no, I'm going out for lunch." He nodded and she beamed even brighter.

"Okay. I'm going out and wanted to know if you needed me to wait for the delivery."

'No, you can go, that's fine." He looked down at his phone and picked it up, sent Keily a quick message to say he had a meeting, and grabbed his keys. "I'll see you out, shall I, Monica?"

"That's very kind of you, Logan."

Monica's tall frame nearly filled the elevator as they went down to the first floor. She was a large woman, but not intimidating. Not to him anyway. He couldn't say the same thing about how his other employees felt about her. All she had to do was look at them sometimes and he'd hear them gibbering on about whatever they'd come to ask her. It always made him smile.

Keily had learned to be the same way before she quit, a talent that meant he wasn't disturbed when she knew he was busy. And there he was, thinking about her again.

He didn't have a meeting to get to, he just wanted out of the office. He stopped at a fast-food place and then went out to drive around the place he now called home. The views didn't grab his attention, and all he could think about was Keily. With a frustrated sigh, he drove out to a park and ate his lunch in silence.

A love song played on the radio and he wondered if that's what was wrong with him. Was he in love with the one woman he shouldn't be? He had no idea what romantic love was, not really. He knew what the movies said it should be, he knew what a crush felt like, he'd had one whopper of a crush in high school, but was that love? He'd barely known the girl he'd had the crush on, so could that be love?

Was love needing to see someone? Be with them and hear them laugh? Or was it wanting them to be happy, even if that meant you weren't in the picture? Was love mowing the grass and taking out the trash without being asked? Or was it candy and roses? The card writers of the world wrote about need and happiness, was that love? Or were all of those things rolled up into what love actually was?

He and Keily never talked about love and he steered the conversation away from anything that might end with the word 'relationship'. He was having an affair with her; he'd insisted that to himself from the beginning. An affair wasn't a relationship, it was purely sex. Right?

But it wasn't just sex that they shared. They watched Netflix together and actually chilled. They discussed the shows they binge-watched, and news, politics, all the things that people in a relationship should talk about. Well, maybe not everything. They didn't talk about their pasts, their families, or their hopes and dreams. Those were matters they both avoided.

He'd set her up as his mistress, the same way men had for countless generations. He gave her a home where he would be king, provided her with an income, and bought her gifts. She was his mistress and an exceptionally talented one. She could be a skilled courtesan in the world's royal courts. Henry the Eighth wouldn't have looked twice at Anne Boleyn, he knew, if Keily had been in his court.

That meant that Keily would lose her head, he thought with a frown. He didn't want to behead her, at all. Now, getting head from her, that was a different matter. That made him smile, until he realized he was smiling idiotically. She'd turned him into some kind of soppy douchebag, which was another reason he'd avoided her this week.

No, he thought decisively, she was his mistress, and considering anything else would be a mistake. Keily might make a politician a good wife, and she was great with his clients, but he didn't need a wife. He'd never thought about having one, or kids, and didn't want to think about either now. He wanted to be able to focus on his business and get through his day without worrying about what some woman needed.

Which he did, despite himself.

"Fuck." He spit out and started the car back up. He was on fire, burning up into ash, for a woman that would be no good for him.

Keily wasn't the woman he needed in his life. She was exactly what he didn't need. Selfish, greedy, morally ambiguous in many ways. But... was she really?

Perhaps in the past, but not so much lately.

She'd become kind, caring, a thinker who obviously considered her past actions. She didn't ask him for anything, except his company. Even that she only asked for in delicate ways.

This wasn't how he'd planned any of this to go that day when he'd seen her application on his screen. None of it had gone as planned. Keily was a force to be reckoned with, even if she no longer had the greedy look in her eyes. Even if she didn't even say she liked him.

She did, he heard it every time she said she hated him, the words that meant exactly the opposite hid in her eyes, in her voice. It was in those unguarded moments when she purred out those spiteful, hateful words that he found he needed her the most. Because she wasn't telling him she hated him. Not at all.

She purred those words so beautifully, in their most heated moments, when they should be saying other words to each other. That's when they both admitted what they still managed to keep hidden. The word love was never spoken, but hate was something they could both admit comfortably.

Maybe hate was just a word that meant love when you couldn't actually say that word. When love had been rejected, hate was the only thing that could replace it, right? There was apathy, of course. He considered it for a moment, but knew apathy wasn't right at all. Hate wasn't either.

Was he truly capable of...that other thing?

His eyes narrowed as he drove back to work. He focused on the road, but his thoughts were still on Keily. She took all of his self-control, even if she didn't know she did. He wondered if he did the same to her? Did he make it impossible for her to think? Were her nights filled with dreams of him? Were her days spent pining for the moment he came in her door?

Is that what that message really meant? Not that she would find something else to do if he wasn't coming, but that she was on the edge of breaking down and demanding he come to her? She wasn't the kind to do that, to admit she was so weak she needed his company. But was he her weakness?

It was a possibility.

And insane.

He walked back into his office but changed his mind. He walked over to the plant to have a look over operations. He talked to the employees, whether supervisors or packers, machine operators, or forklift drivers, and that took up the rest of his day. It kept his thoughts off the one thing he shouldn't be thinking about at all.

As he was driving back home at the end of the day, he looked at his phone expecting more texts from Keily. There weren't any and he hated to admit he was disappointed. The problem was, he was disappointed. She'd been a little distracted in their phone calls lately, as if she was troubled but didn't want to talk about it.

He would never push her to talk, even if he wanted to. He wondered what was bothering her, but maybe it was just that business with her mother and her scholarships. She'd talked about it a little, told him that there were funds somewhere that she hadn't touched and that her mom had stolen some of it from her. He'd wanted to ask why she hadn't pressed charges against the woman for theft, but she *was* Keily's mother. That was probably why. No need to ask when the answer was obvious.

Chinese food arrived at his house an hour later and he sat down in front of the television but couldn't find anything he'd want to watch without Keily. Logan blew air out slowly between his lips and stared at the screensaver. He'd been sitting there so long that the screensaver had come on, but he didn't care. He had a problem.

A huge one, even if she was a little bitty thing.

Was he in love with the woman?

He couldn't be. Could he?

Maybe it was time to call this all off, to end it and get on with his life. He could go back to California now, put someone in charge of the place and get back to his real life. Find another mistress.

That idea revealed another truth he didn't want to admit to. He only wanted *Keily* as his mistress. He couldn't imagine coming home to anyone but her. He couldn't imagine even going to sleep beside another woman that wasn't her. Fuck.

This was trouble. A lot of trouble and he had no idea what to do about it.

He thought about it some more, considered never seeing her again, and tentatively probed his feelings about that. What he found was worrisome. There was an ache in his chest and his stomach at the thought. An ache that turned to pain the longer he thought about life without Keily.

He'd thought it would be easy to dump her and get on with his life when he started the affair, when he finally gave in to his lust for her when she quit working for him. He'd fuck her for a week, maybe a few, and then he'd get on with life. That had been the plan. Unfortunately, he hadn't planned on how much he actually…liked her.

She was funny when she wanted to be, sexy, sensual, beautiful, and showed him with actions what she couldn't say with words. She'd made it her business to find out what foods he liked the best and she made them. She bought him gifts too, little things like a robe that was soft, warm. Things that family, or a wife, would buy. Things he'd never consider buying because they were things he usually didn't think about.

She'd bought him soap, razors, even socks. All were little things, but they had all pleased him because they were bought with care. People might think socks and soap weren't really gifts, but to Logan, they were.

Those gifts had touched him more than a brand-new Maserati would, because Keily had thought about what to get him. She'd been at the store and decided he needed things like that. She wanted to meet his needs and he wasn't sure there'd been anyone to do that for him in a long time.

Not that he'd have let anyone else do it after he got out of high school but that wasn't the point, was it? Or was it? A frown marred his features as he got up and walked over to the windows to stare out at his property. Lights illuminated sections of the front yard, but he didn't really see any of it.

He'd go see her again, then make a decision. Maybe that's all he needed, one more dose of her?

If she'd stayed that little minx full of avarice and greed, he'd have been able to let her go a long time ago, but she hadn't. She was actually a human being and a decent one at that. Did she deserve to be treated like a child's toy, to be discarded when he was done playing with her?

Not really, but she knew the score. She could have asked him to be more open about what they were, but she hadn't, and he'd taken that for silent agreement. Maybe she was still acting, only she'd become better at hiding the more distasteful parts of her personality?

Now, that was a thought. Little Miss Keily might have become a really good actress. He doubted any actress could fake the way she came though. That was something that a man who paid attention couldn't mistake. Any man that actually bothered to pay attention would know if a woman was faking it or not.

She loved sex with him at least.

The rest though? Could that be faked? He supposed it could be, if the person wanted to fake things like that. Hmmm.

He thought he was the one in control, the one dominating the situation, but was that true? The way he stood there, all twisted up inside, trying to decide whether to end this or not told him something huge. Keily might just be the one in control after all and that simply wouldn't do. He had to take the control back, one way or another.

9

Keily

Keily expected a sky-high hotel with a view of the beach and some palm trees, concierge services, and a lot of noisy tourists. She was in for a surprise. They flew to the US Virgin Islands on a private plane, took a boat to a smaller private island, and then ended up in the most beautiful house on a hilltop where they could see the hazy shapes of other islands and blue water all around.

The house was painted white with blue shutters, a light and breezy place full of windows and glass doors to let the light in. Orange terracotta tiles on the roof protected the inside of the two-story home that Keily instantly wanted to live in forever. When she saw the bedroom had a glass door she was in heaven because the ocean was right there, she could look out at it from the bed.

The scene would be beautiful at night, with the moon shining over the water, she just knew it.

"Do you like it?" Logan asked softly, his eyes on nothing but her as she walked through each room.

"It's beyond anything I could have imagined, Logan." She answered in an off-hand way, too distracted with looking out at the water that almost every room put on display at the back end of the house. The front gave them a view of the island the house was nestled on, an island owned by a friend of his, he'd told her. They must be some friend, Keily thought while she ran a hand over the granite countertops in the kitchen. It truly was a heavenly place, and she knew their time there would be good.

"There's a pool off to the right of the house, and we have our own boat if we want to go to the bigger islands around here." He told her and went to find a bottle of water in the fully stocked fridge. "I made sure we had everything we'd need, though, so if you want to just stay here for the entire time, that's fine too."

"I'd like to see the whole place, if we have time." She turned to walk up to him, a smile on her face that she couldn't stop, even if she'd tried. "I thought we were going to a hotel, but this is so much better."

"You aren't the kind of lady that would like a hotel, something tells me." Logan pursed his lips but then smiled. "You might, I take that back, but I knew you'd love this place."

"How long are we staying?" Keily tilted her head and waited for his answer.

"I'm not sure yet. At least a week, maybe longer. It just depends on how things go back home." He took the lid off his water and took a drink.

Keily took out a bottle of fruit juice and went to sit in the living room. There was no wall separating the two rooms, something else she liked. The place was just open, and now that they'd opened the doors and windows, a cool breeze blew in to take away the afternoon heat.

Logan gave all his employees a week's paid vacation for Easter, to show his appreciation for their hard work at both of his facilities. He'd come over the night before and told her to pack a bag and get ready for a long trip without telling her where exactly they were going. He'd just smiled until they got to the airport and they boarded a private airplane. That's when she found out where they were going.

It was warm back home, but this place was at least 10 degrees warmer, so she was glad she hadn't packed anything for cold weather. "There's a pool?"

"Yes, and there's nobody else on this island, so you can swim naked if you like." That grin of his, that devilish one that made her knees want to turn to jelly, spread over his face and his eyes gleamed.

"Oh, now that sounds like a good idea. After something to eat first. We missed lunch and I'm starving." Keily got back up, headed to the stainless-steel fridge, and opened it up again. "Looks like a sandwich is the only thing I have the patience to make at the moment."

"I'll make it, why don't you get settled and head out to the pool? I'll bring it out to you."

"You're pampering me?" There was something pleased in her that made her smile girlish, even if she was a grown woman. She could feel it as she looked at him, standing there in black shorts and a black t-shirt, black sandals on his feet.

"I might be. Go on now, get relaxed. Six hours of traveling is a long day, we both deserve a rest."

There was a softness to his voice that made Keily pause for a moment, her eyes searching his face. Logan could be funny, authoritative, even nice but sweet and soft? That wasn't something she was used to with him. Turning away, she hid the frown that marred her features and walked to the bedroom they'd chosen on the second floor. Something was up with him.

Wind blew the white cotton curtains gently

against the walls with a soft rustle, but it didn't bother Keily. She liked the sound and looked forward to sleeping in such an oasis of comfort. Amongst other things, she thought with a smirk as she removed the tiny denim shorts and white tank top she'd worn on the journey. On anyone else, the outfit would have looked less than classy, but on Keily? She knew she looked the epitome of class, especially with some of the expensive accessories he'd given her over the last few months added to the ensemble.

In the past, that would have mattered for her own ego, to make her feel above others but now, it was all about making sure Logan looked good. That meant the woman on his arm had to make those that looked at him wish they *were* him. Even if he still wouldn't call her his girlfriend.

Keily took off the jewelry next, grabbed a towel big enough to cover the bed from a linen closet she'd discovered in the bathroom earlier, and headed out to the pool. It wasn't massive but the aqua-colored water was enticing. Nestled in between trees and the hillside, the pool was square, dropped off at one end to create a waterfall effect, and looked out over the ocean. It was, in a word, amazing.

Dropping the towel, Keily walked into the cool water, instantly quenching the heat on her skin. It had been hot in South Carolina, but this was heat fueled by humidity that created a haze around the islands in the distance. The cool water felt like heaven and she never wanted to get out of it. Logan said they were here alone on the island, which meant it didn't matter that she was naked in the pool, completely free as she floated on the surface of the water.

She floated there for ages, her mind blank, body sprawled out, until a voice intruded on her peace and she startled to an almost crouch.

"Now that is one very fuckable body." Logan chuckled as she glared at him. "It's a shame you're hiding it."

"You scared me, asshole." She muttered but then changed her glare to a smile designed to seduce. "Coming to join me?"

"Not if you're going to call me an asshole and glare at me." Logan's eyebrows came down and his mouth pursed.

Was he pouting? She almost laughed at the idea but lifted an eyebrow instead. "You kind of deserved it, scaring me like that. Maybe I don't want you in the water with me now."

"There's one thing I know about you, Keily, more than anything else, and that's the fact that you want me, any time you can have me." Logan's frown eased into a devilish smile that made her heart race and her nipples go tight.

She wasn't going to give in to him so easily, not yet.

"If that's what you think, Logan." She swam to the other end of the pool, the deeper end, and put her arms up on the tiled edges to stare at him. "I think the opposite is true, I think you want me any way you can have me, any time you can have me."

Her intense gaze was a dare. A dare to prove her wrong, but it was also a dare to prove her right. She so wanted him to prove her right, even if she couldn't admit that out loud. Only in her mind could she admit such things, things that she'd never dare say to anyone, especially him. That would give him too much power over her.

"You'll never know." He muttered as he put his hands over her shoulders onto the edge of the pool to hold his body against her. "But you'll want to."

He wasn't wrong.

"Tell you what, why don't you go in, have a little rest, get showered, and then I'll take you somewhere really..." He paused to run a finger down from her right eye all the way to her chin, captivating her with promises he'd never say out loud "...nice."

She couldn't breathe, not when he was looking at her like that, not when her heart was racing so fast it felt like her lungs couldn't keep up. All she could do was nod and climb out of the pool. He really fucked with her when he did things like that.

For a moment she could have sworn there was more than lust in his eyes and she hated herself for it, but she wanted to see more of that. She wanted to see this Logan that was always so in control unable to hold in emotions that neither of them was supposed to feel.

She was in so much trouble. She'd known that for a long time, but this sealed it. She was in over her head, but she didn't want to get out of it the same way she'd climbed out of the pool. For once in her life, Keily wanted to take something more than material things. She wanted to take something that might be...love?

All she could do was shrug as she wrapped a towel around her body and headed into the bedroom.

Losing her head now would be a mistake, she thought as she headed into the shower and let hot water rinse the chlorine off her skin. It was impossible to get him out of her head, but she tried as she rinsed the soap off and then got out.

Where was he taking her tonight? she wondered to distract herself. He'd suggested she rest up, so did that mean he was taking her out to dance or something? It wasn't something they'd done before, but there was always a first time for everything, right?

She sprawled out under a cotton sheet that was probably more expensive than some people's televisions and tried to relax enough to fall asleep. It was impossible though and the only thing that happened was the sun went down a little more. Logan made slight noises in the living room, but they were so faint that she wouldn't have heard anything if she'd actually been asleep. With a resigned sigh, she reached for her phone and pulled up a book to read.

She didn't realize she'd fallen asleep until Logan came in to wake her up with a gentle touch on her shoulder.

"Wake up, sleepy head." He smiled down at her and all she could do was smile back.

"Time to get ready is it?"

"Yep, time to get ready. Might I suggest that black dress you brought, the lacy strappy one with all the crisscrosses in the front and back?" Logan made a motion with his hands that made her laugh softly.

"Sure, I know which one you mean." He'd advised her as she packed her suitcases, suggesting also that they'd probably pick up a few things while they were here. "The black heels too?"

"As if there would be any other choice." He winked before he went into the bathroom to shower.

She had no idea where he was taking her but that didn't seem like a bad thing.

So far, she'd seen luxury beyond anything she

could possibly imagine, even as Joe's wife and a pageant queen. Logan's life was all about having what the have-nots couldn't even dream about. What he had planned for tonight could be anything, but she at least knew it would be something amazing.

10

Keily

"It's a sex club?" Keily whispered loudly, stunned as they walked through a closed-off entryway, through a door, and into a scene out of a porno. Or a brothel, maybe. Or perhaps, some filmmaker's idea of what a sensual, lavish, over-the-top orgy from a bygone era would look like. Either way, it was more tasteful than she'd thought a place like this would be.

"I suppose it is, yes," Logan answered, his hand on her back to guide her through the open doorway and further into the dimly lit area where scenes were being played out that Keily just couldn't take in all at once. He put away the card he'd held up to a camera at the entrance as they walked deeper into the large, open first floor.

The house was some kind of historical home that had been converted to showcase the different areas people congregated in with separate beds, curtains, and other accouterments every ten feet or so. Or maybe it had always been a brothel. Kiely looked over at Logan, surprised, a little confused, but also...curious.

On the first floor, open all the way to the end of the house, in front of each 'room' separated by curtains or thinly latticed bamboo walls, there were areas for sitting with chaise lounges, couches, ottomans, and coffee tables to hold drinks. Floor lamps had been placed in key positions, to keep the room from being completely dark but did little to fight off the gloom. That didn't mean Keily couldn't see though, because she could observe everything that was in view and she wasn't bashful about looking. To their left was something that looked like an old-fashioned study, the walls lined with books, a desk, and even an antique globe that took up a massive amount of space.

For now, Keily ignored the people in the room in various states of dress and continued to look around her. A bamboo lattice wall separated the library/study from a sitting room that featured a roaring fire, Edwardian-era satin-covered sofas, and a grand piano. Her eyes flashed on to the next room and here she settled on the people, not just the decoration.

This room was a kitchen with appliances that looked as if they came straight out of a post-World War II era catalogue and the people inside were dressed in similar costume. At least, the women were. The four women, in various stages of undress, would be suitable to grace any pin-up calendar from that era, right down to their hairstyles. Luckily, there was no food cooking in that room and the only heat came from the bodies inside.

Keily's eyes lingered on the black-haired woman who sat on a black granite effect Formica countertop with another woman kneeling between her legs. Keily couldn't see what the other woman was doing because the first woman's skirts covered the other woman completely, but if the blissful look on her face was anything to go by, Keily knew. Her gaze remained there, remembering Rosa's words from a few weeks ago. What was it like to be that intimate with a woman?

Keily thought the answer might be intriguing, but she didn't really want to find out. She was there with Logan and even the tall, dark-haired man with steely gray eyes that looked directly at her couldn't distract her from him. He was completely naked, that man thrusting into the woman in a black and pink poodle skirt over by the kitchen sink. He pulled back enough to reveal that the woman wore a black garter belt beneath the skirt and Keily reminded herself to buy some of those at some point.

She'd never watched people having sex before, never thought it would be something she'd participate in, but this was...exciting. At first, she was a little shy, but now that she'd had time to look around and saw that everyone was having a good time, she wasn't so upset. "What is this place, Logan?"

He took her hand and guided her to the stairs that led them up to even more rooms, these with curtains that were opened or closed. He took her to a room with a huge balcony that was accessed by a tall sliding-glass door. White lace curtains billowed in the breeze, but Logan brushed them aside as he led her out onto the balcony. The ocean met her eyes this time, not sex, and the ever-present noise of the water ebbing and flowing soothed her.

"It's as you said, a sex club. Everyone in there is a willing participant, it's not a place for prostitutes if that's what you're wondering, and no we will not be participating with any other people. I just wanted to show you a different side to life." He stood there, not touching her, just letting the words sink in.

"But...what if we wanted to participate, if *I* wanted to participate?" She looked back at him, waiting, watching for his answer. She felt the way her nostrils flared and saw his own do the same.

Anger marred his features for a second, then his brows dipped in consideration. "No, no participation. You're mine when we're here. And I'm yours. When we're here."

"Right." She pulled both her lips between her teeth and turned back to the black cast-iron railing. "So, we're just here to observe."

"That's all." He agreed from behind her, so close his voice made a shiver run down her spine. He still didn't touch her, but she knew he was there.

"But, Logan, I don't get it." She turned to face him, not sure why he thought this was a place to bring her, even though he said it was just to see another side of life. "How is watching sex supposed to be...enjoyable?"

"Ah, you haven't watched long enough, that's all."

"If you say so." She answered doubtfully but didn't turn away. She did, however, stare at the tiled floor of the balcony. "Shall we go back in, then?"

She didn't want to admit she wasn't simply confused with him; she was confused by herself. The man downstairs with the woman wearing the garter belt had been cover-model handsome. She'd been intrigued by the two women as well but hadn't wanted to participate with them because she had Logan. But at the same time, she was curious.

What would it be like to be with two men? Or another woman?

Wasn't that why he'd actually brought her here, to introduce these ideas to her? All men had fantasies about being with two women. Didn't they? That could happen here, if he let it. Or she allowed it. He didn't want that, though, so she'd follow his lead. As always in these situations.

"Of course," she finally answered him, her eyes back on his face, searching for answers she knew she'd probably never get.

Was this just another way of showing her that she was just his sex toy? The thought nagged at her as they went back down the stairs and to a section at the front of the house that she hadn't noticed. There was a bar there and from the smell of it, food was available too.

"Do you want a drink?" He asked as he looked over the bottles of scotch on display.

"Just some water, please." She replied without a second thought. She wanted to keep a clear head, even if the noises and sounds in the open space threatened to overwhelm her with fascination.

She turned around to look at the other rooms, the ones she hadn't looked at before. The nearest 'room' was about ten feet away from them and the only furniture in there was a bed. A full-figured blonde woman's hands were tied with black silk scarves to each of the posts on the headboards, but she wasn't being subjugated. Rather, it looked like she was being pleasured to within an inch of her life. There were four men on the bed with her and Keily would have thought it disgusting in a previous life, now though, she let her mind open up and watched.

One of the men was between her legs, obviously fucking her. His body was powerful, his skin a dark brown that stood out against her pale white skin. Two tanned men, knelt beside her, sucking at her nipples, their hands busy between her thighs. The last man knelt over her, feeding her his cock, which she seemed hungry to consume.

Now *that* looked like something she wouldn't mind giving a whirl.

Keily didn't notice that she'd walked closer to the group, didn't notice that her breath was coming fast, or that she had her hands balled at her hips. She watched them with a fascination she didn't think possible.

"Jealous, are you?" Logan's voice was a breath against her ear. She couldn't look away from the group on the bed, though, even with his nearness to distract her.

"Maybe." She still gave a slightly petulant answer, just to keep him on his toes. "What woman wouldn't want to be at the mercy of four men when their sole aim is to please her?"

She'd always assumed scenarios like this were

degrading, meant to subjugate the woman, to break her down to little more than holes to probe. That's not what was happening here, though. Not at all.

"I suppose I see your point. Let's go down to the last room."

Keily had noted small sofas spread around the path that led to the stairs, but it only occurred to her now that the sofas were for watching from afar. "Couldn't we just sit here for a moment?"

"Is it that interesting?" He sank down to the emerald green satin sofa, a perplexed look knotting his dark brows together. He turned curious brown eyes to her that burned with so much intensity that she could feel his gaze as she sat down beside him.

"I always thought it would be...dirty. Degrading, you know? I heard things when I was in high school, you do when you're a cheerleader and you date the captain of the football teams. Boys wanting to 'run trains' on you and shit like that. So gross." She paused to shudder as she remembered some of the cruder comments she'd heard over the years. "But that..."

She waved her hand at the woman now groaning as her body knotted up in pleasure and looked on with envy. "That looks amazing."

"I didn't know that had happened to you." There was a note in his voice, like he'd just discovered something he didn't like, but made him see her in a different way. "I always assumed life was perfect for cheerleaders and the other popular girls."

His tone now was thoughtful, and she knew that he wasn't actually seeing the scene he was looking at but thinking.

"Don't worry over it too much." She added, not wanting to break the spell of the place. Especially not to discuss things she'd rather not remember. "It's all in the past now."

"But sometimes, we can't leave our pasts behind us." He spoke so softly she barely heard him.

"It's fine, I'm fine. I got over it and you've shown me something I didn't know existed, that things like this happen. Even in pornography, it's always the male gaze, the male's needs that are being met, the women are just there to be fucked. But this is something else. Do you think they're a group?"

"A group? Like polyamory?" He turned back to look at her. "You know about that?"

"Well, I don't live under a rock, Logan, now do I?" She gave him a playful smile that made her eyes dance. "I just thought things like...*that*...would always be about the men."

"I'm sure it is, sometimes, but it doesn't always have to be." He rubbed at the back of his neck before he continued. "I've been to a few places like this before, my friend that owns this place owns a few more back home, so I've seen a lot of wild stuff.

But it's not always as terrible as some pornos make out. Not all men are monsters."

"Okay. You're right. You aren't, so there's you. And those guys over there." Her curiosity was slaked now that the woman was finished, and the group was moving off the bed to dress. "Shall we continue?"

"Indeed." Logan got up immediately and took her hand to help her up. "I'd suggest we go back upstairs, but some of that is...kinkier than down here."

"Kinkier how?" She moved to the next couch and saw the next room was another bedroom, a man and a woman were fucking up against a wall, the woman blindfolded, the man biting into her neck in a way that looked painful but had the woman moaning loudly.

Pain as pleasure, not an idea she hadn't contemplated, or even explored a little with Logan, but that would hurt tomorrow, that bite mark.

"Leather, whips, handcuffs. That kinkier." Logan said breezily but didn't look at her.

"Are you into that?" She asked quietly as they moved on, the next room somewhat brighter than the others.

Logan looked down at her with a look on his face that reminded her vividly of something from her past. In particular, the look her father would have on his face when he played a song by Tonic that was called *If You Could Only See.* Her dad would go into the garage and play the song while working on his lawnmower, over and over, every time there was an argument with her mother or when her mother did something terrible. She heard the song often.

It was a look of despair strangely mixed with hope, but her memory of her father's face lasted longer than the look did on Logan's. It was gone before she'd thought her last thought, replaced by a confident, tilted smile.

"Nah, not my scene at all. Although, having you tied to a bed for a while does sound like fun. But without all the whips and chains." He winked as he leaned closer to her with that rakish smile that made her willing to do anything he pleased.

"Then I'm not interested in going up there, Logan." She leaned into him, her eyes pleading for a touch, a kiss.

He obliged and gave her both. His tongue found hers quickly while his hands cupped her breasts, and it wasn't long before she wanted to climb over his lap to kiss him deeper. So that's what she did.

Logan broke away, his dark brown eyes surprised but not unpleased. "You sure you want to do this here?"

"That depends on you, Logan. Do *you* want to do this here?" She made sure the dare she'd given him earlier was back in her eyes. It might be a dangerous game, but where else should such a game be played?

He'd brought her here for a reason, she wasn't about to back down now and play the scared little innocent who didn't want to have a good time. She wanted to experience everything he wanted to show her, and maybe a little more if she dared to be greedy. She'd lived the life she was supposed to up until the point when she got divorced. Now, it was time for her to have a little fun. Who better to have that fun with than Logan?

Keily glanced around, saw some people behind them coming to rest on a couch. Next to them, in a room decorated entirely in pink, were two women, no men at all, watching her, waiting for...what?

Keily narrowed her eyes at them, saw the one with black hair and brown eyes wink at her, and smiled back. That wink told her it was alright to have a little fun, to enjoy the moment, to take part in something many people would never be brave enough to try.

She caught sight of the couple on the couch again, a strong, handsome man and a petite woman, getting to her knees and unzipping the man's pants. Was she about to get a show of her own? Keily watched, waited, as the woman revealed the man's length and took it in her fist. Keily was impressed, but it wasn't as impressive as Logan's. She looked up at the man, caught his eyes, and felt her entire body come to life. This man would watch her, his gaze promised, if only she'd stop fucking around and get to it.

The woman's head turned to stare back at Keily, a smile on her face that promised so much more, if Keily continued to watch. The woman must be dressed as a flapper from the 1920s if that black headband and long black ostrich feather meant anything. She wore nothing but black stockings, a garter belt, and a bra that was little more than black strips of cloth sewn to frame the outer edge of her breasts while leaving the flesh out in the open. A rather sexy ensemble on a woman with deeply tanned skin and sky-blue eyes. Keily watched the feather as the woman ducked her head down to taste the man she held in her hands. Only a taste.

The man, the near double of an English actor that had starred in a series about street gangs from the 1920s that Keily loved and another one about subjects that were quite forbidden, stared over at Keily, his gaze steely, but full of the same kind of daring as the woman's. The same as Logan's eyes had held. He wanted her to participate, he wanted her to be brave, and the slight smile that tilted up the corners of his lips told her he knew she was about to give in. When he opened his mouth in a gasp of pleasure, Keily nearly lost it. There was sensuality in that gasp, uncontrolled pleasure that enticed her to join him in the land of the forbidden.

But did she really dare?

She'd dared a lot of things with Logan so far, to the point that she might be in a lot of trouble, at least emotionally. Would this be a step too far? Would she be able to walk away from this and be the same person?

The man didn't move at all, even when the woman's head began to move on him. When she saw the slick traces of the woman's attentions on the hard length of the man's cock, Keily involuntarily licked her lips. They were all waiting for her to decide what her fate would be. Boring old sex in a pool or something a little more daring.

For a moment, Keily could have sworn the fingers on the man's right hand twitched. Beckoning her over to him? Or to the dark side of life?

She didn't know, but she wanted to find out. She was more positive about that than she'd been about anything else in her life. She wanted whatever this night brought her, whatever Logan gave her, and she wanted it all.

"Well?" She asked, her eyes back on his face, her eyebrow up again. Maybe she could dare him into making the decision for her. What would be the fun in just capitulating, after all?

11

Logan

"Such a tease." He muttered as he slid his hands up the back of her smooth thighs to cover her silk-covered ass. He gripped at her flesh tightly, cupping her into his erection, so she could feel just how willing he was to have her right there, in front of anyone that might be watching. "Are you sure *you* dare?"

"I don't back down from dares, Logan, you should know that by now." She answered pertly, her left eyebrow arched in challenge. "And bringing me here? Showing me around? That was about as big a dare as you could throw down."

Fuck, she nearly undid him every single time she looked at him like that, and she was always, *always,* looking at him like that.

"But are you sure? There are people strolling around now, watching, waiting to see how brave you are. Are you brave enough, Keily? Can you let these strange men see your breasts, for example?" He cupped her breasts through her dress, rolled them in his palms, but she didn't look away. "Can you bare them for the other women to see?"

"Is that what you want? To have all these people watching me while you fuck me?" She paused, her lip caught between her teeth for a moment. "Or do you want them to watch you, Logan?"

Logan glanced around, caught the eyes of a redheaded woman with a tantalizing amount of cleavage pressed into an emerald green corset. She leaned against a wall, alone, her right index finger in her cleavage. Logan gave her a brief, almost imperceptible wink before he gave Keily his full attention once again. Let the woman watch, if that's what got her off. "Oh, it's not about me at all, Keily. This is your experience. I brought you here for you to have fun. I'm just in the crossfire of whatever you decide. The question remains, though. Are you willing to let these people see your naked body, even your most intimate places, as you fuck me? Because, by the look of it, they will be watching you, Keily."

"Oh, I think you know the answer to that, honey," Keily whispered and pushed her breasts into his face with a subtle breath.

"Don't think you're going to make me make this decision, sweetheart. It's all up to you. You say yes, we fuck right here on this couch, with an audience. You say no, we go back to the house and I fuck you in the pool. Either way, I'm fucking you tonight. The choice of where is yours."

His fingers gripped her ass tighter when she began to kiss him like she was trying to consume his face. He didn't protest, he just matched the pace of her tongue and rocked up into her heat. When she moaned with delight, he responded with a groan that made her whimper. If he wasn't kissing her, he'd have grinned. She was trying so hard not to answer, to make *him* make the decision, but that wasn't how this worked. Not right now, anyway.

He distracted himself while she ground down on him, needing desperately to calm his libido down. His thoughts turned to the other men in the room. They would all see that it was him, Logan, who had the once-high school cheerleader sitting on his lap, riding the ridge of his cock. Him that had her all but begging him to fuck her. He'd been the kid nobody paid attention to, the bookworm too busy studying for parties and shit like that. He'd had a crush here and there, but nothing he acted on. And there'd been the bullying he tried his best to avoid.

None of those assholes would believe where he was now, or who he had in his lap. None of them would know what it was like to have the full-grown taste of Keily as a wanton needing to be fucked, not like he did. They could watch, they could see it, they might even be able to hear and smell her desire, but they'd never know what it was like to feel her, not until he was done with her. And even then, he doubted any man would fuck her the way he did. He knew exactly how she wanted it, when she wanted it, and what buttons to push, because he'd paid attention, learned, and waited for her to teach him.

Despite those thoughts, that wasn't what really drove Logan right then. Instead, it was a fascination with the woman brave enough, confident enough to let him fuck her here, in this place made for sex. Sure, it was kind of obvious what would happen, but still. She could have balked at the entrance. She could have demanded he take her home.

Instead, she wanted him to show her off, to show off himself. To fuck her until they were both senseless, with an audience that was a mix of the seen and unseen. Logan knew there were rooms upstairs, rooms where people could watch without being seen. They'd be looking at his Keily too.

"Pull your top down a little." He demanded, and she obeyed, exposing her breasts as she tucked the top of the dress and the cups of her bra under the round globes. The material of the straps that crossed her chest created a frame around her breasts, created a picture that was sultry and inviting. "Good."

He made her wait, his lips barely against the sensitive tip of her nipple. Her body was telling him that she was aroused, that she wanted him. The dark red flush to her nipples was all he needed to see to know she wanted him. Her nipples gave her away every time. When she wasn't aroused, they were a dark pink, but when she wanted to fuck? They were almost the color of red wine.

The thing that really set him on fire was that she didn't try to hide her bare breasts from the others in the place. She was focused only on him and as far as he could tell, she didn't care that anyone else existed. Only he existed for her, and that was something he didn't know he'd even wanted.

"Hmm, not yet." He whispered softly and stood up with her wrapped around him. "Get down. No, don't pull your top back up, leave it as it is and lean over the couch. Yes, like that, Keily."

He knelt down behind her and heard her gasp when his lips touched her ass. He slid her panties down her legs and glanced around to see what she looked like. Her breasts dangled out of her top, inviting anyone to touch them, to tease her into something more. Her skin was flushed there too, a deep red that showed off just how excited she was.

"Don't move, Keily. Just stand there." He ran a finger up her leg, admired her calves, pressed into shape by her high heels, and let her wait an agonizing ten seconds. Once he'd counted to ten, he pushed her dress up over her hips to run his tongue between her thighs. He nudged at her inner thighs with his thumbs until she opened further, letting him deeper into the treasure hidden there. He wasn't going to get her off, only drive her as high as he could before she got there.

"Fuck, people are watching us, Logan." She whispered, but it didn't sound like a stop to him, so he kept going. His tongue delved into her, tasted her, and filled his head with her scent. The moment was all about her, about driving her to a wildness she hadn't experienced before. "Fuck, they can see me."

It still didn't sound like a protest, so Logan continued the tease until he found her clit. He stopped there, her ass high in the air and bare for anyone in the place to see, and lashed at her just the way she liked it.

"You're going to get me off if you don't stop." She warned, but he didn't listen. She wasn't there yet. She hadn't begged him to fuck her. She wasn't nearly there yet.

He heard her gasps, her moans, and waited, waited for that one sound, that hitch in her throat that was always the signal. The second he heard that sound he moved, brought her back down to his lap, and brought her face to his so she could taste herself on his lips.

Thoughts of the past and where they were at present disappeared when she reached between their bodies, undid the dark blue jeans he had on, and pulled his cock out. She could have just gotten off riding the ridge of his cock through his pants, she'd done it before when they were at home and she was more than ready for him. But now? She'd had him on his knees in public, had his tongue inside of her, and she wanted the full experience.

"Don't stop, fuck me here, Logan. Fuck me now. Please." She breathed as she shifted a little and sank down onto him, completely bare, and he felt how slick she was on the most sensitive flesh on his body. Some of that was from him, he knew that, but most of it was her juices, her arousal that turned her walls into liquid gloves that surrounded his cock with wet heat.

Keily purred as her body opened for him, took him. All Logan could do was hang on and take her nipple in his mouth to spur her on. It was impossible to keep his eyes focused on her now, but from the way she clenched around him, he knew she was fully invested in this. She didn't want him to stop.

Her body moved to a rhythm only she knew but he let her have her dance. He sucked at her nipple, inhaled her scent, and tried not to let go too soon.

His own arousal didn't matter right now. Only Keily mattered and she was close, she was too excited not to be. He decided to tease her a little more.

"Do you see them, Keily? All the people watching you fuck yourself on my dick? Do you?" He paused but she didn't answer, she just grunted a little and kept riding him, her hand digging into his shoulders as she moved on him. "They all want to fuck you, or be you, you know that, don't you? Even I'm in awe of you and it's my dick you're bouncing on."

"Fuck you, Logan." She gasped but couldn't say anything else, not when her head was back, and he had her nipple in his mouth again.

He wanted her to be louder though, to let it all out, and he took her other nipple between his fingers. She didn't last long once he'd latched onto both nipples. Her walls gripped at him, tantalizing him to join her, but he held back, waited, watched as she threw her head back in total surrender.

Everyone had to hear the way she groaned now, they all must be watching, but he wasn't worried about looking. He heard the responses of others in the room, heard the moans, the groans, the sudden inhalations of male and female voices as pleasure was sought and found. Keily's voice joined theirs again as a growl of pleasure, and this time, Logan groaned too. She was almost too much temptation.

This was what he wanted now. He wanted Keily just like this, at every possible moment. It was all he'd wanted for a long time, but he'd held himself back, away from her, away from most people. He'd almost left her at one point, afraid this part was coming, but he'd hesitated, and now? It might just be too late.

Her back arched suddenly and she moaned long and low, but he felt what was happening, knew that she was letting go. He held onto her, kept her on his lap as pleasure made her head fall back, strangling the groan of pure bliss that wouldn't be stopped. Her hips didn't stop moving, didn't stop riding him at all as he waited for her to finish.

When she pulled back to take her nipple from his mouth and pulled his face up to kiss him with sensual gratitude, he lost the will to control himself any longer. He whispered words into her mouth, words she wouldn't hear as she kissed him. Words he didn't really want to hear himself as pleasure took over and melted his brain into nothing but Keily.

He was totally fucked, but he didn't care. Not anymore.

All that mattered was Keily and how good it felt to be inside of her.

12

Logan

*H*e was going to have to go jerk off or something if she didn't wake up soon. He'd woken up in the middle of the night, the memory of their time at the club earlier in the evening still lingering in his thoughts. Kiely was asleep, but not for long. He whispered her name against the back of her head as he ground his hard length into her.

He'd fucked her as soon as they got home earlier, but the need was there again, raw and real, deep in his mind, not only his body. He wanted her again, and he'd have her if she let him.

Keily gave a soft whimper and her hips moved, instinct taking over as she felt his need, even in her sleep. He'd woken up hard as a rock, memories of watching her ride his dick in such a public way still fresh and exciting. Something about the wildness of her passion still drove him, even in his sleep. He needed to stamp his claim on her again before the dawn rose and reality intruded.

"I need you, Keily. I need you wrapped around me, taking every inch of me, the way only you can do. Please, Keily, wake up and tell me I can fuck you." He was desperate, and nearly lost control the moment he felt how wet she was against his fingers. "Keily, tell me to stop if you have to, but please, wake up and tell me something."

She didn't answer verbally, but the way she pushed her ass back against his erection told him all he needed to know. With a twisted smile, he slid his fingers to just the right slick place and pressed harder. Not too hard, just enough to make her moan.

"Are you going to make me beg, Keily?" His lips whispered the words softly into her ear, loud enough for her to hear and to shudder as he teased at her clit. "Is that a yes? Because I really need it to be a yes. You know that."

For a moment at the club tonight, Logan had noticed a man looking at Keily, looking at her with lust, with greed that Logan didn't like. But then Keily had explained. She locked eyes with the man while she fucked herself on Logan's dick. She stared at the other man the entire time she fucked

Logan, the woman with the man going down on him until he exploded in her mouth. Logan didn't want to share her with anyone, but what she described, what he'd seen in that man's eyes, still made him achingly hard.

"Yes, Logan. Please. I need you to fuck me, to fuck this ache away." Her words were a murmur that eased his mind, soothed his fears, and made him want to growl like a possessive caveman. Even if he wasn't a caveman. Or possessive. At all.

Logan slid her right leg back to his to open her thighs to him before he slid between her folds. She had to do a little maneuvering, but he was soon as deep inside of her as he could be. Every inch of him that she could take was inside her, filling her, and he loved the way she took him. "Fuck, I love this, Keily. I love being inside of you."

He didn't care if she answered, or if she took his words the wrong way, he just had to say them, didn't even realize he'd said them out loud really. His mouth moved in time with his hips, telling her how much he adored fucking her, how he never wanted to stop, as he drove them both higher.

Being inside her blunted the worry that she might have wanted to fuck that other man, made him realize that she only wanted the voyeuristic thrill of it, of knowing that fucker wanted her but couldn't have her. Because she was his.

She wasn't about to do a disappearing act on

him or trade him in for a different rich guy that would fuck her brains out. Not when she had him to do the job right.

He rocked into her with measured strokes until she dug her nails into his hip. "Logan, make me come, baby, please."

The power he held in his hands in that moment made him stop. He wanted her to beg him for more, he needed to hear her say...something.

"You're thinking about that man, aren't you? The one that watched me fuck you? The one that wanted to be you, Logan, to fuck me the way you fucked me." Oh, how she could tease him when she wanted to. She could draw that power right out of his hands and into her own. But at the same time, she gave that power back freely. "I almost wish he'd been another you, a clone, so that I could fuck you both. Or suck his dick while you fucked me. Because only you get to fuck me, Logan."

He thrust into her, harder, not ready to answer her. It was such a filthy idea, but he had to admit, he'd love watching her suck him off while he fucked her at the same time. Even if it was also confusing, and weird, it still made his cock throb as he thought about it. "You can fantasize about whatever you want, Keily, so long as I'm the only one that fucks you. Or fucks that beautiful mouth of yours too, I might add."

"Then don't stop, Logan. Fuck me harder." She

dug her nails into his thigh again, not gentle at all, but he didn't care. That pain was exquisite pleasure.

It was one of those moments he'd worry about later, but in that instant, he didn't care. His bare cock was inside of her, sweetly wrapped in her slick velvet walls, and she was handling him like she was born to do nothing else. He hesitated, waited, knowing that she'd give him a little more, if only he waited a moment longer. She'd break and plead with him again.

"Please." She sighed softly and that was all he needed to totally lose the last shred of his control.

Logan moved her onto her hands and knees, slipped out of her long enough only to slip back inside her from behind before he ground into her again. Maybe she'd driven him insane with need, but he didn't care. She was his, and his alone.

He hated that she had any kind of power over him, hated that he wanted her with a need that made him feel weak. But he couldn't get her out of his head. Even when he tried to.

She drove out every thought from his mind, even when he was at work and needed to focus. She made it impossible to make decisions that would dictate his future, but he couldn't care. Didn't care, especially when he was inside of her.

He'd been a loner all of his life, even as a child. When he grew up relationships had been all about power, business, and control. Even the women he'd fucked had been chosen based on what he wanted from them. A night of sex, nothing more. It wasn't like that with Keily, and fuck if it wasn't a problem. But he didn't care.

"Logan, don't tease me." She begged, pretty in her need.

He did exactly the opposite. He strummed at her clit and whispered to her, still inside her as he spoke. "Keily, my sweet Keily, you want to come desperately don't you?"

"I do, Logan, I do, please." The words choked off as he stroked her again, with just the right amount of pressure.

"But you can't get that man out of your head, can you? The way he looked at you, the way he wanted those beautiful nipples of yours in his mouth. Because that's what he wanted, honey. He wanted to touch you, taste you, fuck you. But he can't because you're all mine."

He couldn't believe how his own words made his dick throb as he waited inside of her. It made him grunt with amusement that masked his plea-sure. "Do you really want me to fuck you hard, Keily? Are you sure?"

"I am sure, Logan, I am. Hard." Her face was smashed into the bed, facing the sea view, but she didn't see any of the view right now. Her eyes were closed in concentration as he circled her clit with a touch that was a little too soft, a little too...delicate.

He pulled at her left hand, brought it between her thighs as he grabbed her hips and gave her exactly what she asked for. Rough, deep, and fast.

She didn't complain, she opened up more for him instead, pushed back against him, met each thrust with one of her own. "Just like that, Logan, just like that."

He could only groan as he plunged into her, watched the sensual arch of her back in the moonlight as she moved with him in perfect time. His fists tightened on her hips, wanting to hold her still as he fucked her, but he didn't want to bruise her. Logan loosened his grip, but she held still anyway. She went on instinct when it came to sex with him, and her instinct told her to give him what he wanted, and she'd get all she could handle. He'd learned that much about her. She wasn't a stupid woman, after all.

He groaned with total bliss when he felt her clench around him when he pulled her up to cup her full breasts. Breasts that other man had wanted in his mouth. Wanted but couldn't have. Only Logan got to tease those hard nipples as she circled her clit with her finger, as she ground down onto his dick, kissing him hungrily the entire time. She might very well be the best fuck of his life. He knew she was because he couldn't get enough of fucking her, but admitting that out loud wouldn't be something he'd do any time soon.

He let her have her fun, let her drive the pace, he was happy enough to have her wet and hot around him. His hands were full of her breasts, teasing at the stiff peaks of her nipples, remembering the way he'd stared up at her as he emptied himself inside of her earlier. How good it had felt to fill her as she watched him for that split second. She'd looked up, away, to that man and the woman who'd been busy pleasuring the guy with her mouth. She'd come before Logan had a chance to get even a little bit soft. He'd wanted to continue to fuck her, but now was as good a time as any.

"Come for me, Keily. Show me how you do it." He knew she loved the power he'd given her, knew it by the way she moved her hips, the way she nearly collapsed when his arms tightened around her.

She gave a soft hitch of a sound, and then he felt it, that first flutter of her desire. Her head went back, against his right shoulder, pushing her breasts further into his hands. She filled all of his senses, surrounded him with her touch, her smell, her sound as she came hard and long in his arms. For a moment, he felt as if he was one with Keily, one soul, one human, one form, as he lost the will to hold back and followed her into oblivion.

He pulled her face up to his, used his fingers at the joints of her jaw to open her mouth, and kissed her with ravenous hunger. Pleasure coursed through his brain, his body, as she moaned into his mouth and pulsed around him. He filled her with the flood of his release, without a second thought, with any thought, other than how good it felt to come inside of her.

Logan sucked in air through his nose as the kiss continued long after his balls had stopped pulsing and she'd slouched in his arms. The kiss wasn't about sex anymore, it was about emotions he didn't want to name, thoughts he didn't want to think.

Keily let him have his moment, gave it back to him. If he knew her, and he did, she was probably having the same overwhelming rush of whatever the fuck this was as he was. She pulled back a little and Logan opened his eyes. He saw it there, that same panic, that same knowledge, the same 'oh fuck' that repeated over and over in his mind. But there was also something that might be happiness in her eyes. Was it in his as well?

She slipped from his arms and went back to the side of the bed she'd chosen. He faced her, wanting to watch her in the moonlight. He didn't think, pushed away the thoughts that told him this was all a mistake, that he needed to take her home on the first plane back tomorrow. He forced his brain to be quiet and just enjoy this moment of peace with her.

He'd been alone for so long, it was nice to have her company, even when they weren't having sex.

Okay, so they didn't have deep meaningful conversations about their pasts, but they did have talks about other subjects. She was knowledgeable in areas that surprised him, business, politics, comedy. Who'd have thought that she'd like comedies? He wasn't sure why he'd assumed she'd hate them, but he had. They even talked about films, documentaries, art, and the future hopes he had for the company. Just not about a future together, or their pasts.

Logan could only guess she didn't like to talk about Joe because the guy was a drunken dickhead. What else did she need to say about him? She never mentioned him, almost as if he'd never existed, unless Logan brought him up or to ask about the court case.

She didn't mention her little sister anymore and he knew that was a sore spot for her. He brushed a tendril of hair back from her face and smiled at her. "Good night, Keily."

"Good night, Logan. Wake me up if you have that in mind again." She murmured with a sleepy smile.

She didn't mention her parents anymore either. She'd almost become this self-contained box that spoke only about topics he wanted to talk about. But he wasn't sure he liked that. He wanted to know more about her, wanted to know the things that worried her, that made her sad.

But…

Did he?

Would that be the safe option? To deepen their relationship?

He rolled back onto his back and closed his eyes. A cool ocean breeze blew in through the window, drying the slight sheen of sweat on his skin. Would he be able to blow her out of his life as easily as that breeze blew in the window if he knew all the things he wanted to know?

It was a quandary best left to another day, he decided. For now, he'd enjoy the time he had with her on the island and worry about tomorrow another day. He deserved the peace, for once in his life.

13

Keily

"This sucks. I wish we were back on that island." Keily groused as she picked up her phone and thought about calling Rosa.

The other woman was at work and it wouldn't be a good time to call. Especially with Logan so... grumpy lately. He wasn't grumpy with her, but Rosa let her know that since they'd come back from their vacation, he'd been a bear to deal with at work.

Today wouldn't have made things any better, either.

They'd been back from their vacation for a little over three weeks now and Logan had to go to another court appearance that morning. Keily hadn't gone to the courthouse because Logan hadn't wanted her to come and because she hadn't been needed. They all knew Joe's attorney would continue the matter as many times as the judge would allow, and they weren't wrong. She'd had a text from Logan at lunchtime telling her just that one word and nothing more.

"Continued."

She rolled her eyes and put the phone down.

She wondered, not for the first time, what had changed on that trip that left him so damned irritable all the time now. They'd had a good time, there'd been a lot of sex, a lot of laughs, and even some exploration of the islands. It had all been really good, she thought, a turning point in what could be and what might be.

The news from Rosa made her wonder, even if he was the same guy when he was with her. Maybe the problem was at work, and not something personal to Logan. Not that he'd talk to her about it, either way. He wasn't the kind of guy that talked about feelings or emotions, or even the past. Every now and then he'd talk about the present, but normally, they didn't have very long conversations about him personally. Logan had a way of turning the conversation around to her, even when she made a point of asking him something about himself.

He'd arrive soon, so she went into the bedroom, freshened up her makeup and hair, changed into a slouchy t-shirt dress, and put some lasagna she'd frozen into the oven. That was something else she did now, prepared food and froze it. Her days were so empty she didn't have much else to do.

Which reminded her, she needed to find out about those scholarships. She'd decided to call some of the pageants too, find out exactly what prizes she'd won and lost. Back then she hadn't really paid attention to prizes and things like that, she'd been focused on winning and little else. She'd found out when she was younger some details of what she'd lost, but now, she wondered if there'd been more. Wasn't there a car at some point?

She'd just hit send on an email to one of the pageant organizers when Logan knocked and came in the door.

"Hey, dinner smells good." He opened his arms as she stood up from the couch and walked over to him.

"Need a hug?" She asked before she could draw the words back in.

"I think I do today. I don't know how you stood being married to that man for so long." He grumbled a bit but kissed the top of her head. "I have to give you more credit, just for that."

"Well, a lot of self-delusion and playing an ostrich did the trick most of the time." She scoffed as she pulled away and went to check the timer on the oven to see how much longer the lasagna needed. "It was when he dropped his pants on live television that I finally had to admit a lot to myself."

"I guess we all lie to ourselves about some things, sometimes." He answered carefully. "Salad?"

"Yes, it's made and ready to go out. This has a few more minutes and it will be done." Time had flown while she hunted down pageant organizers and emailed them. "Fresh French bread or do you want me to toast it with garlic?"

"Fresh is fine." He answered. "My mom used to make me lasagna on the weekend and freeze it, you know? She made a lot of meals for me, then she'd freeze them, and I just had to bake them when I got home."

"Oh?" She answered just as carefully, wanting him to go on, but she also didn't want to push. He'd just clam up, she'd learned that much about him.

"Yeah, she worked first shift, so she'd be home, but most of the time, she'd be so tired after a day working in a plastic products factory that she'd go to bed exhausted. It was really hot in that place. Dad worked at the same place, but on second shift, so I rarely saw him either. We did have a lot of plastic cups and straws though, I have to admit." He laughed a little and began to set the table.

"Oh? There used to be a plastic factory here somewhere. I think it shut down years ago though. Everyone said it was like working in hell." The timer went off on the oven as she spoke, and she went about pulling the tray out.

"It could be, especially in the summer. It was more tolerable in the winter. They live in California now, up north in the mountains. They love it there."

"Oh, that sounds nice. I've heard it's beautiful up there. Over there. Or is it both?" She looked at him as she set the lasagna on a placemat and went back to get the salad and some dressing from the fridge.

Logan grabbed the French bread from the counter and took it to the table to cut it up. "Both, I guess. It's nice. They have a house up in the mountains, a swimming pool, and their privacy. They're happy."

"Do you see them often?" She prompted, hoping he'd go on while she served the lasagna onto plates. He never talked about his family.

"They worked hard when I was a kid and I rarely saw them. When I had the money, I bought their house for them, help them out every month, but we were never really that close. I go see them once or twice a year." He shrugged and took the plate she offered. "Thanks."

"My pleasure." And it was, hearing him talk about himself for a change was a real pleasure.

"No siblings?" It seemed a strange question to be asking all this time later, but that's how Logan preferred it. Now, he'd opened up a little and she wanted to see how far he was willing to go.

"No, they were smart about that. They had me and that was enough. I'm not sure they even wanted me really. Not that I pity myself or anything, it was just they never really seemed to care if I was around, you know? I'd go off and read a book or play something on the computer and they'd leave me in peace while they did their own thing. They had me right out of high school, they didn't even know who they were yet, so I guess it's not that big of a surprise they realized they didn't really want a kid after all."

"Hmm." She paused, thinking about everything he'd just revealed. He'd had a lonely childhood, felt unwanted by his parents, and had little contact with them. And he thought they didn't want him. "Maybe they just thought they were respecting your privacy?"

"Maybe." He answered and they both went quiet while they ate.

Keily didn't want to lose the moment though and as she took her last bite, decided to try another question. "I think it's different with boys, you know? Parenting? With girls parents are always trying to teach us how to be proper young women, and all that cooking and cleaning nonsense. With boys it's motorcycles, playing outside, learning how to fix cars and lawnmowers, things like that. I bet they just thought you were doing what you wanted to and left you alone to do it."

"Maybe." He repeated, but then shook his head. "I think they were just too tired, most of the time. Dad worked even on the weekends when he could, so he paid a guy to mow the grass, and Mom was always cooking meals on the weekend, and reading in bed when I came home from school. Even during the winter months, when it was cooler, she'd make meals on the weekends, so she didn't have to bother during the week. Or she gave me money to order pizza or something."

"It doesn't sound like the happiest of childhoods." She mumbled, picking up their plates to wash the dishes. "I guess we both had shitty parents to deal with."

"I have to say, your mom sounds a lot worse," Logan replied, going to put the leftover lasagna to cool on the stovetop and put the salad away. "Mine didn't steal from me, at least."

"Oh, I forgot I told you about that." She felt her cheeks burn and couldn't look at him. She *had* forgotten she'd told him and now she was ashamed of her mother. "No wonder I turned out to be such a bitch, right?"

"Nah, you're not a bitch, Keily." He stood close to brush hair away from her face with solemn eyes and a soft smile. That soft smile turned into a huge grin before he spoke again. "At least, not anymore."

"Oh, you bastard!" She pushed him away gently and handed him a dish towel. "Dry the plates and shut up."

"Yes, ma'am, but then I have to go. I have to make a call later and I can't be here, being distracted by you so I'm heading back to my place. That okay?"

"Sure, yeah, it's fine. I'll call Rosa, have her come over." She nodded but felt disappointed. She'd miss him but knew if he stayed, he'd have her naked and they'd both forget the world existed.

"Thanks for dinner." He said once they'd cleaned up and put everything away. "I hate to go, but I have to make that call."

"I understand and it's fine." She walked into his arms, kissed his jaw, and rested her head on his chest. "I'll see you tomorrow?"

"Probably." He said without conviction.

She didn't comment on that, just called Rosa to come over so she wouldn't be alone. Luckily, her friend joined her without hesitation. It was while they were on their second glass of wine that she got a reply from one of the pageant organizers. Her mother had turned down the car in lieu of a cash payment. A cash payment that Keily never received from her mother.

"Um, girl? Don't you think your mother should pay you back for all this stuff she stole from you?" Rosa asked, her eyes on the email Keily showed her.

"I don't know. Can you have your mother arrested for theft?"

Rosa eyed Keily with pity and doubt in her eyes. "Would you really press charges?"

"Now that I'm adding it all up, seeing how she's still not clean, and doesn't even care that she screwed me over? Yeah, I kind of am."

"I don't blame you and whatever you decide, I support you." Rosa nodded her head, her lips pressed flat in a grim line.

"I don't know what I'd do without you," Keily answered and leaned against her friend, dressed in a summery peasant dress of cherry red cotton that Keily adored. "Does that mean I can borrow this dress?"

"No, but I can tell you where to get one of your own." Rosa laughed and hugged Keily tightly.

"You're such a good friend." Keily joked back, but as she slipped her arms around Rosa's waist, she really meant it.

14

Logan

"*F*uck me." He muttered a week after he'd spilled his guts to her. She was a picture of summer seduction as she came out the door dressed in a knee-skimming cherry red peasant dress that fell subtly off of her shoulders, a pair of matching red heels on her feet. There was even a thin, patent red leather belt around her waist.

Red. The color of passion, ardor, love, and most of all...lust. And how he lusted for her.

The heels weren't a color he'd have chosen, not from any of the choices he'd seen online so far, but on her? They were perfect, as was the dress.

"Wow." He said as she let herself into the car and slid down into the passenger seat.

"You like it? Rosa got it for me." Keily smiled her wide, pageant-winning smile at him, ready for a night out with one of his clients.

He knew she hated the dinner meetings, but she was a good sport and played along.

"Yeah, I love it. And you're getting a tan, too." He waited until she had her seat belt on then pulled the car out of the driveway.

"Thanks, all that time spent around the pool during the day reading, and in the evenings with Rosa." She took a deep breath, looked around, and turned to him. "Where are we going?"

"Some place that makes buffalo wings the client likes. Willy's Wild and Wily Wings." Logan paused to shudder. "Not a place I'd choose, but that's where he wanted to go."

"Probably to stare at the girls. It's not Hooters, but it might as well be." Keily laughed and put her arm on his right thigh. "It's not bad, at least the buffalo wings do actually taste good there."

"I guess."

They'd been sitting at the restaurant for fifteen minutes, had already gone through two glasses of iced tea, and were getting annoyed by the time the client called Logan.

"Hey, buddy, listen, I got a family crisis I have to deal with. Can we meet up tomorrow?" The client, a man named Jim, asked and Logan had to pull the phone away as a woman screamed in the background. Something about two-timing man-whore and then the sound of glass shattering.

"Uh yeah, you deal with your crisis, Jim, and we'll get in touch when you're ready to talk."

"Thanks, man. Gotta go. Bye."

"Cancelled, has he?" Keily asked, sipping her tea innocently. But the way her lips wrapped around that straw wasn't innocent at all.

"Not a totally bad thing, I have to say." Logan moved around in the bench seat, trying to ease the pressure of his pants over the erection that had sprung to life as he watched her full lips sipping sweet tea.

"No?" A flirty eyebrow crooked over her eye and she got that look on her face again. That one that dared him to do things he knew better than to do. "Want to eat here?"

"Yeah, I saw a burger on the menu that'll do. Then we're going home."

"Sounds like a plan." She answered, moving closer to slide her hand over his leg before she gently cupped his balls. "The getting home part, that is."

"We could always leave, order something...at home." He really wanted her to take him up on the offer, especially when her thumb grazed over his cock beneath the table, her other fingers still cupping his balls.

"Sounds like a great idea to me." Before he could

reply her hand was gone, she grabbed her bag and stalked over to the register to pay their bill. It was only for a few drinks, so he didn't protest.

Besides, the impression of her hand on him so intimately made it a little hard to stand up. He took a deep breath, waited while she paid, then stood up to leave with her.

"Maybe we should have stayed there. Ever since that night at the club, I've thought about all the things we could do in public, without getting caught that is." She leaned over towards him but didn't touch him. "I know I've said it a thousand times since then, but I loved that. Knowing anyone could see us, that people *were* watching us."

She'd told him about that couple that sat on the opposite side of the room, facing them instead of the little 'rooms' set up in the sex club that night, when they first arrived back at the house and when he'd woken her up to fuck her again. Apparently, the woman of the couple bent down to give the guy head while he watched Keily fuck Logan. And she'd loved knowing the guy wanted her, that he hadn't taken his eyes off of her while his woman had sucked him dry.

"There's nowhere around here like that. I can take you back to LA next week, maybe, if you want to do it again." He offered but knew she wanted something now. That thrill of being out in the open, of anyone being able to watch them.

An idea formed, one that had him turning faster than he should have to take the road to his house. There weren't many cars that came up that way, and they'd have privacy. He slowed the car to a stop before he got to the house. "Get out."

"Oh my." She said but didn't complain.

"Get in the back seat, lie down with your feet on the running boards." He told her, an order more than a request. "But take your panties off first."

Blood was already throbbing through his veins, urging him to get inside of her as quickly as possible, but he wanted this to be good. He watched her quickly pull her panties off and toss them on a floorboard before she did as he asked. He walked over and noticed his knees would be on the gravel path if he knelt down now. "Scoot back a little."

Keily let her legs fall open as she did as he asked, ready to take what he wanted to give. He didn't say anything, just positioned himself the best he could and moved to position his face exactly where he wanted it, over her glistening folds. She was excited already, ready for his touch. "Tell me what you want, Keily. Tell me and I'll make it happen."

He would too, he'd give her just about anything, within reason.

"I want to be watched again. I want that so much." She panted even though he'd already slid his tongue into her folds and up to the spot that should make her speechless. He didn't mind. It was her fantasy; he'd let her tell it however she wanted to. Even if that meant she'd end up breathless and panting. That was, of course, his goal.

A quick glance up showed him that her face was flushed and she had the heel of her left hand pressed against her eyes, to block the world out as she relived that moment she couldn't seem to forget. He knew she really loved watching the woman with the group of men. He knew it was something she'd probably explore in her mind, but she wouldn't speak about it again, not unless it was in front of them.

The man watching her though, that had set her off too. She'd told him more about the guy the next day, as he fucked her in the pool. She'd whispered about the stranger until she came harder around him than he'd ever felt her come before. He had a feeling that was about to happen again.

He distracted himself with thoughts of how Joe had repressed her sexuality for all the years they were married. Okay, he didn't want to admit to himself, or anyone else, that they were in a relationship, but he wanted her to explore what got her off, what aroused her, and what made her feel like a woman. He wouldn't share her with anyone, not even another woman, but the rest...exhibitionism, voyeurism, that he could explore with her.

He'd just ignore that whole question of why he didn't want to share her, he decided as she plunged a hand into his hair and started to grind against his face. She was almost there. Her words now were mere rambles of things she remembered, things she wanted, and he tried to pay attention but he couldn't, not when she tasted so good and uttered those small cries that made his cock rock hard.

He wanted to just push his pants down and plunge inside of her, but he had to wait, he had to take his time. Let her have her fun. And she did with a loud groan, just as her back bowed and her thighs clamped around his ears. He continued to tease her clit until she pushed at his head, too sensitive for his touch now. The second she did that he pulled away and pulled her out of the car.

"Come here." He mumbled and bent her over the hood of the car, her ass bare as he pushed the skirt of her dress up over her back. She didn't complain or protest, she just took a stance that would allow him to get inside of her and not fall over.

Even the skin on her bottom was tanned, with no lines, so she must be breaking some rules when she was alone in the apartment complex during the day. He liked it and stroked his hands over the silky skin and around to her hips as he lined up with her entrance. They both sighed when he sank into her without any resistance.

"Anybody could see us here, Keily. Anybody could come up the road. They could even be watching you right now, ready to slide into you just like I'm doing. Wishing they fucking could, but they can't because you're mine." It was the only time he'd admit it, the only time he'd say it, really. But she didn't complain, she never did.

"I don't want anyone but you, Logan." She answered, her breath halting as he plunged into her slowly but deeply every time. "I only want you."

It was the one and only time she'd ever say those words to him, when they were fucking, and he knew she meant them. She'd said them before, as she came, when she wanted him to let her get off at last after teasing her for far too long, pushed to the edge, but now? She said them freely and without him pressing her.

Did that mean she meant them?

For a while, he'd been toying with the idea of breaking it off with her. He'd told himself a thousand times to let her go, to find someone else to slake his lust with. Women were freely available to good-looking men with big dicks and bigger bank accounts. He could crush her, at last, as he'd planned all those months ago when he'd hired her to be his personal assistant.

He'd wanted to crush her back then, to see that fiery confidence die and wither into shame and disgrace. But...it might be too late. He'd forgotten that plan for a little while.

It was getting harder to think those ideas now,

the more he learned about her, the longer he stroked into her. He never wanted to be anywhere but inside of her, whether that be in her mouth or any other place she chose to let him enter. He simply loved being in her.

"Come here, Keily." He ground out and pulled her up. He didn't care if it dented the hood of his car, he wanted to look into the gray eyes he couldn't forget while he fucked her. She obligingly hopped onto the hood and pulled him into her. "Fuck…"

It was a sigh of pleasure as he slid back into her. Somewhere in the back of his mind, he knew he really needed to stop fucking her without protection, and he never did when they were at her apartment, but then there were these unplanned moments that were risky, but so worth it.

"What's your fantasy, Logan?" She looked up at him, that tease in her eyes again, gray and clear. "Fucking me on your car? Fucking me with an audience?"

She was closer to the truth than she knew, but he shook his head. "Just fucking you, Keily, that's all I care about."

"Good thing you get to do that whenever you want then, isn't it?" She moved her hips in time with his, grasped at him until she had a grip on his biceps. She liked clenching things, him especially.

"It is, Keily, it definitely is." He could only grunt

now as sweat dripped down his back from his exertions in the heat. He wanted her to come again, but he was losing his grip on his control.

She did that to him, left him totally exposed, even if she didn't know it. Wanting more of her, unable to walk away. That had been the plan, but he hadn't counted on actually liking her, coming to admire her. He hadn't counted on just how amazing Keily really was, once you got to know her.

And she hadn't exactly had an easy life, although he'd assumed she had. Cheerleaders always smiled when he was in high school and he'd assumed that meant they were always happy. She'd told him that was an illusion and he'd believed her simply by the cold look on her face.

But now he didn't care about any of that. Not when she pulled the top of her dress down to bare her breasts to him, not when she squeezed him, drawing him deeper inside her walls. All he could do was hold on as she took him for the ride of his life and hope that later, sometime much later, he could get back to his plan. Maybe.

15

Keily

"What have you decided?" Rosa asked, lying next to Keily on a sun lounger on a quiet Sunday afternoon. It was June, the sun was hot, and the pool was the only place either of the women wanted to be.

"About?" Keily hedged, hoping Rosa wasn't asking about Logan.

"About your mom," Rosa said bluntly, her sunglasses and wide-brimmed hat hiding her face.

"Oh, that." The question about her mom wasn't any easier than talking about Logan.

"Yes, that. So?" Rosa turned her head to look at Keily, but Keily had her own hat and sunglasses on.

"I haven't decided anything yet." Keily squinted to see her friend but even with the shade of the hat and her sunglasses, the sunlight directly behind Rosa glared down and hid the woman's features.

"It's a tough situation, my friend. I don't know what I'd do either. No pressure, just wondering if you'd decided anything." Rosa turned to the table to her left and picked up her bottle of water.

"I can't believe everything she took. Stole from me, really. I didn't know about most of it. I thought it was just the stuff I found in her drawer back when I was in high school, but it wasn't. She even sold trips if the tickets weren't issued in my name. That's all I got, some of the money to buy the things I'd need for the pageants, dresses, makeup, that sort of thing, and the things that were issued in my name that were non-transferable. That's it, after all those years."

"And the scholarships." Rose pointed out and for once, Keily smiled.

"Yeah, it's a relief that I can use those. I wish I'd known about them before I split up with Joe."

"What are you going to study?" Rosa asked and turned onto her stomach to tan her back.

Both women wore identical tiny black bikinis, barely clothing at all, because they'd both loved the style and ordered them online. Keily thought Rosa looked much better in hers, and for once, wasn't jealous of another woman looking better than her. Rosa was her friend, a beautiful woman, and Keily could admit that without a qualm.

"Oh, I've already started classes. I'm focusing on a business degree. That should be fairly universal, shouldn't it?" Keily turned over too, her head on her arm beneath her face.

"Should be. You were good at what you did when you worked with Logan and you're a smart lady, I think you'd do great in the business world. And you already know how to make sure people understand you won't take any prisoners, so you've got that going for you too."

"Thanks." Keily smiled, not sure it was a compliment, but since it came from Rosa, it must be.

"And what about you?" Keily asked to get the conversation away from her life and problems.

Violet still hadn't returned any of her calls and texts, and she'd stopped trying while she was on that vacation with Logan. Maybe it was time to give up on repairing that relationship. She hadn't spoken to her mom or dad, either, but didn't really want to talk to them. Her dad went along with whatever her mom wanted, and her mom was basically a thief who'd stolen from her own daughter. Keily was still fuming about that and probably always would. How could you forgive something like that? Knowing her mom had used the money for drugs made it even worse.

"I'm good. Work is fine, although Logan's still in dick-mode most of the time. He leaves me alone, at least. My family is good, and I'm having fun going out with this couple I met while you guys were on that dream island." Rosa let that slip like she hadn't just dropped a bomb in Keily's lap.

Keily's head whipped around and her mouth dropped open. She closed it before she spoke. "Wait, you mean going out, going out, or just going out?"

"Going out as in we don't actually go out a lot." Rosa's face was turned towards Keily now, and despite the glare, she could see the smug satisfaction on the other woman's face.

"I want details, woman, now! How could you keep this from me?" Keily sat up on the sun lounger and grabbed her own bottle of water.

"I wasn't sure where it was going and I didn't want to get your hopes up if nothing happened." Rosa sat up, too, her knees almost touching Keily's. "I wasn't actually looking for a couple, but I met them at one of the, uh, more adult places in Spartanburg."

"Adult places?" Keily asked before the penny dropped. She leaned forward even more and pushed her sunglasses up. "You went to a strip club?"

"I might have." Rosa laughed at the shock on Keily's face and how far her jaw had dropped. Again. "I'm brave since I got divorced, what can I say?"

"How did that work, was the woman working

there or something?" Keily wanted to know everything. Ever since Logan had taken her to that club her brain was hungry for knowledge about all things sexual and sensual. Living vicariously through her friend wasn't a bad thing either.

"I was sitting at the bar, watching the women dance, fending off scuzzy guys that automatically think a woman in a place like that is either working there or looking for a quick fuck. This cute little woman with long black hair and the most dazzling blue eyes came up next to me and told this really gross asshole to leave me alone, that I was there with her. I wasn't going to deny it and once the guy left, she sat with me and we had a few drinks together. She's so cute, Keily." Rosa turned, snapped up her phone, and showed Keily a picture of a woman that wasn't just cute, she was beautiful. And she had the most delightful tilt at the end of her nose that made her smiling face even cuter.

"Wow, she is cute, Rosa. Tell me more." Keily waited while Rosa swiped through the pictures.

"This is Jake, her husband." Rosa held the phone out again.

A man with a charming grin and lots of curly brown hair stared back at Keily with gray eyes and a body that was used to a gym. He wasn't wearing a shirt because he was standing in a pool, obviously at their home, judging by the privacy fence and the brick house in the background.

"Wow, hottie." Keily grinned wider and demanded to know more. "So, what happened next?"

"Well, don't get mad, I know it was stupid, but we went to Waffle House and I met her husband there."

"What's so stupid about that? Other than it was a Waffle House." Keily shrugged.

"Because instead of going home that night, I went home with them." Rosa pulled her lips in and waited for Keily to fuss at her.

"Um. Okay. Not wise, but you didn't die, so something must have gone right?" Keily didn't see the point in fussing at her friend. The woman was an adult and knew the precautions she should take to protect herself.

This was all new territory for Keily, being a supportive friend had never come naturally to her. She'd been taught that other females were her competition her entire childhood, but she liked not thinking that way anymore. It was...freeing.

"No, I didn't, thank goodness. I know it was stupid, but you'll see it when you meet them. They're just so...wonderful. We hit it off right away, all three of us, and nothing happened that night. We just talked until the sun came up. I slept in their spare room, and I went home after break-fast the next morning. I've seen them a few more times since then, well a lot more times, and every time it just feels like I'm, I don't know, home? I think I feel like I'm home when I'm with them. Don't laugh." Rosa held out a warning finger but Keily shook her head.

"No, I think that's great. I think that's how it's supposed to be." Keily sat back on her lounger, her thoughts now on her own life. "Joe never felt like home. I don't think I actually loved him, either. I said it, thought I meant it, but I don't think that was love."

"And Logan?" Rosa pushed lightly, her left eyebrow arched over her sunglasses.

"I don't know. He's been weird lately." Ever since that day when they pushed their luck and had sex in, and on, the car, he'd been...angry?

That didn't seem right. Not angry. Distant definitely. Resentful felt like the right word.

He'd looked at her that day like he wanted to consume her, but also like he hated her for it. Emotions had swept through her the entire time he fucked her on the hood of his car; fear that this was the last time, excitement that she'd conquered him, sorrow that she still felt that way. Worry that he almost looked like he hated her.

"How weird." Rosa finally prompted her when she didn't go on.

"He's just, I don't know how to say this. He comes in, he goes home. He hasn't stayed the night in a long time. I think he might..." She stopped, unable to say the words because her chest had suddenly become too tight to speak, to breathe almost.

"Oh, no, honey. I've seen how he looks at you. He's not done. Maybe he's just got a lot on his mind with work?" Rosa comforted her or tried to.

Keily stared off into space, ignoring the reflections of the water from the pool, as dread overwhelmed her. Pain fluctuated with that dread, pain in her chest, in her heart, that stole her breath away as she thought about life without Logan.

Would she be able to cope with that? She'd known all along that this wouldn't last forever, but she'd started to have the tiniest bit of hope that maybe...

"I don't know." Keily shook herself out of the stupor and took a deep breath. "I just know something is up."

"Women always know." Rosa agreed, no longer trying to comfort Keily. "What can you do?"

"Nothing, I guess." Keily waited until Rosa had sat back on her own lounger to continue. "What can you do and still have some pride left?"

"Sometimes we have to swallow our pride, my friend," Rosa answered immediately, her head nodding. "That was part of the problem with my ex, he could never admit to how he felt. I know things are strange with Logan, but maybe talking to him would help?"

"I don't know. This all started after he actually started to open up to me. Maybe that's the problem, he feels like he has to back off from me now. He's opened up and that probably scares him."

"Maybe so. Men like Logan, they want to be in control, all the time." Rosa nodded again and jumped because her hair came loose from its bun. "Stupid hair, never wants to stay up where it's supposed to."

"Mine doesn't either. That's why I use two hair ties most of the time." Keily laughed, but the pleasure trailed off into a sad smile. "If it's done, it's done, I'm afraid."

"I hope not. You've been so happy with him."

"I have. It's strange. I don't think I've ever been this happy." Even with the uncertainty of what she was to Logan, of knowing deep down that she was just his mistress, even with her plans for the future and her ideas of what she'd do when he grew tired of her a few months ago, this hurt. But even with the hurt, she was happy, because maybe it wasn't done yet.

"Then we'll just have to figure out how to make this all okay." Rosa didn't say anything else and Keily went quiet too, lost in her thoughts.

Two hours later, after Rosa had gone back to her own place, Keily sat in front of her computer screen, staring at a discussion question for class she needed to answer. She couldn't think of where to even start because all she could think about was Logan.

Was he about to leave her?

The screen faded in front of her as her thoughts took over.

She'd started this whole thing with one intention...to be a trophy wife again. She wanted bigger and better than Joe had ever given her, and Logan gave her all of that. The problem was...she'd become bored with being a trophy wife. Well, not a wife but a mistress definitely.

At first, she'd preened and been the perfect companion for dinner dates, glad to be able to eat food from restaurants that didn't put the prices on the menus. She'd loved the expensive gifts, the way he always thought of the perfect things to get her. She'd loved the sex even more, and still did.

What bored her was the uncertainty, the empty days, the nights alone. The awkwardness of not knowing what she *was*. Was she just a plaything that he was about to throw away? Had he already found a new toy to play with?

In the past, she hadn't cared about Joe's little drunken forays into infidelity. She'd pretended she didn't know; he'd pretended they never happened, and they got on with life. Public humiliation had been the final straw with him. Their old friends, people she'd known since high school, stopped calling her. They ignored her on the streets downtown or in the supermarkets. She couldn't handle that, and she'd left him.

Logan wasn't like that. He did things that showed he cared, even if he didn't know it. He took her places, helped her explore life, and gave her new experiences. Life was fun with him, it had meaning, but only when she was with him. Of course, she felt alive with Rosa too, but even Rosa didn't make her feel as alive as Logan did.

Was that love? Feeling alive? Feeling like you were at home when you were with someone? Did being happy mean love?

She wasn't sure about any of it and she had work to do, she reminded herself. Logan would be there later, maybe she'd talk with him about it all, finally. Or maybe not. Maybe now wasn't the time to go rocking the boat. He'd been moody lately, though he didn't take it out on her at all. He was distant too, and that bothered her, but maybe it really was just work. Maybe it was a phase of some kind, something he needed to work through, and things would go back to normal.

It was best to just wait and see, for now. That was all she could really do anyway.

16

Logan

*I*t was the first night he'd stayed over at Keily's in a while. He'd had a lot of conference calls to make to California, some repairs that needed sorting, and he'd spent a lot of time away from her because of it all. Being there beside her, her warm body tucked against his, was nice.

Logan fell asleep quickly, his body too tired from a week of meetings, late-night calls, and working around the house. He'd call someone to take care of the problems at the house, but repairing the broken tiles, the leaking faucets, and cutting down the tree that had blown over in a storm the week before was therapeutic to a man that lived a life of luxury and cold offices. Being able to use his hands for more than signing papers and typing was something he liked but didn't get to do often anymore.

He found himself in the woods, blossoming to life in the spring warmth and filling his sinuses with pollen. He knew he shouldn't be there, dread filled him, and he tried to turn away, to go back in the direction of his lonely home, but his feet propelled him forward. His brain screamed at him to turn back, but his feet refused to listen.

He was 18 again, his hands strong from the manual labor he did over the winter, shoveling snow, chopping wood for the elderly, and any other job he could find to do. He'd been preparing for the days ahead, days that would be paid for with scholarships and his own hard work. He'd need to eat, to pay for other living expenses, and he'd worked hard. But he'd wanted one last quiet walk in the woods before he took off for his new life.

Somewhere in his mind, he knew his graduation ceremony was the next day, and he was leaving the minute that was over with. He was done with this town and ready to get on with his new life. He should be at home, making sure nothing got in the way of him leaving. Instead, he was out here, in the woods, swatting at mosquitoes.

Branches and pinecones cracked under his feet, but he paid them little attention. There was somewhere he needed to reach, otherwise, his feet would turn around and take him back home, right? He heard a sound in the quiet woods, a laugh followed by the pop of burning wood. Now that he'd heard the fire, he could smell the smoke and his heart started to pound in his chest.

Apprehension was a cold fingernail that scoured down his spine as he walked closer, slowly as his feet decided to prolong this moment. He'd been here before, he knew that something terrible was about to happen, but even though his feet slowed, they did not stop. Each step took him closer, until he saw the orange glow of flames, and for a moment, the glitter as the flames bounced off a metallic keychain in the shape of a butterfly.

It was her keychain, the girl he'd had a crush on but never dared to speak to once they got to high school.

"Hey, who's out there?" A throaty voice called out, slurred by alcohol or something less savory. More than likely imported beer. That's what the guy and his friends liked, because the voice was familiar. He knew who it was and knew that he should get out of there. That asshole had been after him for years, though he didn't know why.

Why didn't matter, years of being tormented did and he tried to turn, but instead his legs bowed so that he could kneel down and watch. They were all there, all the bullies and the girlfriends, now taking part in a game of 'find the asshole watching them'.

Sweat broke out over his skin and fear made it hard to breathe. Even if he could run away, could he run from that group? From all of them?

He slid down against a pine tree, not caring that pine sap was sticking to his clothes, gumming up his hair. Someone was running in his direction. He pulled his knees up to his chest, tried to control his breathing, hid his face down against his knees. *Please don't let them see me, please don't let them see me.*

But it was too late.

"Found the fucking perv!" A voice gloated out of the darkness. "I think he's about to piss his pants too!"

There was a struggle, he felt branches digging into his skin on his stomach, then his back, the scrape of rocks against his knees, and he knew what was coming next. He didn't want it to happen, but it happened anyway.

It always did, no matter what he did. He knew it was a dream and tried to wake himself up. Sometimes that worked, but sometimes, the memory of that horrific night would not end, no matter how aware he was that it was only a dream. The pain, the humiliation played out exactly as the night it had happened, without mercy or relief.

He heard female laughter as they dragged him out of the woods and into the clearing near the pond all the kids used to swim in, even if they weren't supposed to. He remembered his parents' warnings about snakes and leeches, but it was the other teenagers in town he needed to worry about. He'd known that all along, but that night made it crystal clear.

"What are you going to do with him? Don't hurt him, he's harmless." That female voice, slurred from the beer she held in her hand, waved at him and he saw that flash again. Her keychain, reflecting the flames, wrapped around her wrist with a soft, baby pink stretchy band.

Fuck, he thought as the guys dragged him over to the fire.

"Well, if it isn't the local nerd. Studying up on how to be a real man were you, *nerd?*" The voice he hated the most spat at him.

There were hands on him again, the girl's voice rising in protest, and then more humiliation coursed over him like a hot flush. Time slowed, sped up, went backward a few times as the dream went on, reminding him over and over of the faint protests, the hateful names they called him, and the way he couldn't escape. Even from the dream of it.

The girl shrieked in protest as one of the boys snatched her keychain from her wrist and held it over the fire with a stick. "We're gonna teach this here boy to mind his manners, now ain't we fellas?"

The accent was an affectation, none of them

really talked that way, but the guy was having fun humiliating his prey. He felt hands where there shouldn't be hands, then cool night air touched the bare skin of his buttocks. He was spread out on the ground, four boys at his shoulders and the backs of his knees, pinning him to the ground. Then a burning pain as the scream he'd tried to hold back finally broke loose from his chest.

Logan jerked up in the bed, covered in sweat and worried he'd actually screamed out loud. Keily slept peacefully next to him, her hand tucked under her cheek while she rested on her side, her face away from his.

He looked down at her, at the angel that she was, and tried to banish the memory. He reached out to touch her, in the hopes that would work, and stroked a lock of her blonde hair. She was the epitome of what all those old masters of artwork painted, from her sweet smile to the wide, guileless eyes. Well, they weren't always sweet and guileless, but in sleep they definitely were.

A feather-soft touch of her cheek, a peck at her bare shoulder, and he still felt no comfort. He wanted to wash away the shame he'd felt that night, because it wasn't only a dream. It was a very real memory, a fact he hid from her even now. She'd felt his ass, but she'd never seen it. She never would, if he could help it.

The knowledge was always there, even when he

didn't want it to be, that he'd been weak that night, that he'd been assaulted but had done nothing about it. He'd run home, put some antibiotic ointment on the burns, the scratches, then applied bandages as best he could. The next morning, he'd stuck to his plan, not willing to let even total humiliation stop him from getting out of that place.

Over the years he'd filled his life with strength, confidence, and chosen a path that led to him heading a company that specialized in selfdefense. He knew that night had put him on that path. He had those assholes to thank for who he'd become in a way. There'd always been a plan in place, a plan that would take him away from his old life and give him a new one, but that night had focused him on self-defense and ensuring others could do whatever they could to help themselves.

That was one of the reasons he quietly donated some of his products to shelters and schools. He wasn't just out to make a buck, but to really help people.

The reminder was just another attempt to kill the memory that didn't work. With a sigh, Logan left the bed, put his clothes on, and left Keily sleeping. He didn't leave her a note or send a text, he just left. He didn't want to be around people once the nightmares started. And one night was all it took for him to endure weeks of insomnia, afraid because he knew what would happen the second he hit that sweet spot of sleep where dreams started.

The drive back to the house was quiet, uneventful, so peaceful that he almost went back to sleep. He was tired, he needed the rest, but he knew what waited for him in dreamland. Years had passed since he'd last had the nightmares. They came when he was troubled, worried about things he couldn't say out loud.

The situation with Keily made his thoughts volatile, left him open to his brain's gleeful torments. No, it wasn't her fault he was so lost in her that it scared him, that he couldn't make himself give her up. But he knew that she was the reason he was all twisted up in knots. A run on his treadmill might clear his thoughts, might help him to get back to sleep. It used to work, sometimes, making sure he was too tired to dream.

He ran for miles on the treadmill, until he could barely stand under the splash of a quick shower to soap the sweat away. While he ran, he played music that usually soothed his thoughts, calmed him down, but he had no idea if any of it would really work. And he knew that apprehension made all the work he'd just done useless, even as he closed his eyes, too exhausted now to keep them open.

It started off as a sensual dream, a dream that was really enjoyable, a dream about the woman he wanted so much he couldn't get her off his mind.

But her seductive smile turned into something twisted, into something nasty as she clamped a hand around his dick and pulled him to the ground from his bed.

He felt, again, the sting of twigs digging into his stomach and cheek, and then came the laughter. That incessant, stupid laughter that he couldn't forget. All of them laughed, all of those guys, as they tore his pants down under his ass cheeks. For a moment he'd been terrified, he'd known true fear, felt it as he bit his cheek, trying to hold back a scream. Why had they taken his pants down?

What were they going to do?

It became clear when the one with the stick held the glowing metal in front of him. A brand!. This was his punishment for taking a walk at night, for trying to hide from them when he figured out they were near. This was what happened when you followed the rules and there was nothing he could do about it but try not to scream.

The scream didn't wake him up this time, he lived through that pain again, the distant laughter that he could hear through his own shock and need for air, air that was strangled in his chest. They'd drifted away, finally, one by one, leaving him there on the ground like a broken toy. He heard female protests again, the mention that he needed help, but a growl to shut up made the girl do just that.

Sitting for graduation the following day was his

next humiliation. Trying not to let on to the others around him that he was in excruciating pain had been a monumental task, but he'd done it. Later, as his parents headed back to the house, Logan had driven away, his ass on fire, his soul in shambles.

He knew he should probably stay off his bottom, that he shouldn't be driving, but he wanted as far away from that living nightmare as he could go. He woke up as the sun rose in his dream, a new day shedding light on his blank gaze and flaccid face.

Logan's eyes opened as the sound of the alarm broke through even the last remnants of the dream. At least he had work to help get him through this. If this was the start of a new dose of hell for him, he could bury himself in work. He could keep Keily and those memories off his mind.

He stared into the mirror as he shaved that morning, seeing a handsome face, a face that men and women both drooled over. But behind that face was the young man that had been too weak to protect himself from bullies, that was too weak now to let go of a woman that wasn't meant for him.

Keily was meant to be a wife, a mother even. Motherhood would suit her, though he'd have never guessed that all those months ago when she walked into his office. She'd been too selfish back then, too self-centered and egotistical. Too hard to show love. Now?

Keily was a new woman, the kind that could be maternal, that could give love, that wanted to give love desperately. He'd seen it in her eyes when she wasn't aware. He didn't deserve her love. Didn't want it, he reminded himself as he finished up with the shave. Men like him weren't meant for love and marriage.

Fucking and moving on, that's what he was meant for and somehow, he had to find a way to break it off with Keily. Find someone with eyes as cold as hers used to be. Someone that could match his black soul with the blackness of their own. Someone that definitely was not Keily.

17

Keily

"*L*ogan's a king in his world, Keily, and you have to face it, you're just a commoner," Rosa spoke as gently as she could, but she made her point.

"I guess you're right." Keily sighed and looked down at her phone. It had been three weeks now since Logan had left her silently in the night. Three long weeks of a text here and there and delivered gifts. Keily didn't want his gifts, she wanted him.

"And stop looking at your phone, it's making me sad." Rosa gestured at the phone on Keily's coffee table with a frown that did little to mar how pretty the other woman was.

"Well, how's your life?" Keily asked, an obvious change of subject but one that needed to be made.

"No, ma'am, we're going to talk this out, and then we can talk about my life." Rosa shook her head and settled into the other end of the couch, her bare feet tucked under her bottom.

"I don't want to talk about my life anymore." Keily knew it came out as a whine but couldn't help the tone. She felt lost, alone, without Logan.

"But you must, my dear," Rosa said, putting on the airs of an old Hollywood actress. "You must release this negative energy and bring positive energy into your soul."

Keily laughed and rolled her eyes. "Stop. He's not all bad, you know."

"I didn't mean he was negative energy." Rosa popped out immediately. "I mean the negative energy he brings to you. The negative responses you have to how much of a dick he is. You know he's a dick."

"But he's *my* dick. And he's not always a dick. I mean, look at all the positive he's brought to King's Hill. This place was dying a year ago and now it's coming back to life. People have jobs, new places are opening up, and it's not all bad you know? He makes me smile when he's with me."

"That's because all you do is fuck, talk about work, and fuck some more. I'd smile too if I had that much sex." Rosa was the one that rolled her eyes this time.

"That's not all we do." Keily protested, but Rosa

wasn't completely wrong. They did have a lot of sex. A lot. But there were times they talked. She was probably the only one in town who knew he was an only child, for instance. "Besides, what do you do with that couple of yours?"

She wasn't about to spill anything that Logan had told her, not even to Rosa. Not about his private life anyway.

"I see you trying to change the subject again, honey." Rosa said with a smirk. Dressed in dark blue denim shorts and a white tank top, she was the epitome of summer fashion in King's Hill.

Keily had on her usual oversized slouchy t-shirt, this time in a sapphire blue with silver stars dotted around it. She'd ordered dozens of them when she found out how soft and comfortable they were.

"I'm not, I'm just making a point. It's not all sex and he's not the ogre you think he is. At least, not to me."

"Then why am I sitting on your couch and not him?" This time Rosa punctuated her point with a lifted eyebrow and pursed lips.

"I thought you liked that I was with him." Keily couldn't figure out why Rosa was anti-Logan all of a sudden.

"I do, I did, but he's causing you pain now and that I don't like."

"Hmph." Keily couldn't argue with that.

He *was* causing her pain. Pain she didn't want to

admit to. She was supposed to be the player here, wasn't she? She was the trophy-wife/mistress that she'd always wanted to be, but turns out, that wasn't the life she'd wanted after all. She wanted more than that and deep down she knew she'd never have that with Logan.

"It's hard to want a real relationship while maintaining your independence, isn't it?" Keily mused aloud, knowing she'd get an answer, whether she really wanted one or not.

"It isn't, not with the right person. Logan gives you the independent part, but not the commitment and that's why you're in trouble now." Rosa leaned over to pick up the glass of wine that was left over from the dinner of delivery pizza they'd shared earlier. "You started out wanting nothing more than what he gave you. The trouble is you want more now. Logan isn't that kind of man."

"He's not, is he?" She swiped at the tears that brimmed over her eyes, angry at herself for getting into this mess. "But stupid me, here I am, wanting what I can't have. Actually, that's not that unusual for me."

Keily had never admitted to how much she'd lied to get the job as Logan's personal assistant to anyone and she wasn't about to now. Still, she knew that lie had led her to where she was now so maybe it was time to rethink her strategy on how to approach life.

"How's school going?" Rosa finally changed the subject, her brows knitted as she looked over at her friend.

"It's good, really. It keeps me busy and I'm working on an idea that I'd like to talk with Logan about, but you know, he's not around." Keily rolled her eyes and took a drink from her glass filled with red wine.

"What is it?" Rosa let the subject change carry on, even if Keily had mentioned the man again.

"It's a self-defense perfume. I've just got to work out a few kinks." Keily went over to get a notebook from the dining table and brought it back. "It would put off a powerful smell if the wearer was attacked, enough that it might convince the attacker to leave the person alone."

"You mean like skunk spray?" Rosa looked doubtful, but she didn't say it was a stupid idea. Even if the look on her face told Keily it was.

"I hadn't thought about that, but yeah, I guess it is. Only you'd always have it on, you wouldn't have to pull out a canister or press a button."

"But wouldn't it activate if you're at a club where it's all hot and steamy, especially if you're dancing? Wouldn't that trigger a response?"

"That's my problem. I have to do more research on pheromones, body temperatures, whether there are differences in reactions to fear or excitement, what if the wearer was in a car accident and had the perfume on? I think I might have to pan the idea, but I thought I'd like to do something that's in line with the products Logan produces." Keily shrugged and turned a page in the notebook. "I also need to figure out if there's even a way to produce a reaction like that with perfume. I don't know, maybe I should just give up and try to find a job as an executive personal assistant again."

"No, don't do that, Keily. Don't talk yourself down from something that brings you to life this much." Rosa's stern voice drew Keily's eyes up from the notebook. "Your whole life people have used you and thrown you away. Nobody has ever loved you. Your parents used you for money, Joe used you as a fashion accessory, your sister used you as a babysitter, and Logan has used you too. For sex. And now he seems to be throwing you away. All of them are the stupid ones if you ask me."

"To be fair, Violet did let me live with her." Keily pointed out, but Rosa shook her head.

"No, honey, she still wanted to use you. Okay, so it sounds like you were a complete and utter bitch to her, but still. You've tried to make amends and she's still mad that you wouldn't babysit. That doesn't sound like love."

"I might have said some mean things to her..." Keily admitted, not for the first time.

"Keily, you're what, twenty-five? What 25-year-old hasn't said mean things? Or am I just hating everybody because it seems like I'm the only person in your life that's ever loved who you are? Who you really are." Rosa reached out with her right hand and took Keily's left hand in hers. "I do love who you are. I love that you're a fighter, that you're independent, and that you're a bitch, but you're willing to learn not to be one and to admit when you're wrong."

"Not always." Keily started but then did a weird little sob-laugh as she looked up at her friend, touched by what Rosa had said. "Thank you."

"Don't thank me, it's true. You're willing to change but you need to stop changing to try to be what you think people want you to be." Rosa let go of her hand and leaned back against the couch again. "You have to learn to be you all the time, Keily."

"I know." Keily sighed and looked away again.

"Don't let him break your heart, Keily, please. I'd hate to see that happen." Rosa said after a quiet moment. Keily glanced up, seeing her own thoughts in her friend's face. It was too late for that.

Her heart was already breaking.

It had never really been broken before. She'd been upset about her parents, Violet, and Joe. But heartbroken? No, she hadn't felt this pain, this fear that she felt after Logan had avoided her for three weeks. Was it over and he just couldn't tell her? She didn't want to think about it anymore.

"Well, you have a late date to get to, so I'll stop blubbering in your lap and let you get home to get ready." Keily laughed a little to let Rosa know she was okay. "Not that you need to do much, you're beautiful as you are."

"You're such a flatterer." Rosa leaned over to hug Keily with a little laugh of her own. "Will you be alright?"

"I'll be fine," Keily answered quickly. Maybe too quickly. She would be though, she had plenty of homework to do and that would fill the quiet hours.

For now, all she could do was focus her energy on the classes and hope that Logan would let her know, one way or another, that this was either over or he'd come back to her.

"I hope so. But, if you need me, call me, alright? I'll come right over. No matter what it is you need." Rosa hugged her a little tighter before she let go and stood up. "I'll call you tomorrow, either way."

"I'll be waiting." Keily stood up to see Rosa out and waved as the other woman walked down the sidewalk.

She was alone again. Alone with her thoughts, her worry, and her sadness. It was eating her alive, this overwhelming feeling of loss. The first week she was able to brush off her worries, able to ignore the niggling feeling of doubt. Logan had left in the night, without a word, but she'd ignored the sting of that until week two.

Now, she was on week three and found herself crying at the drop of a hat.

What the hell was wrong with her?

This being nice thing had taken a toll on her, she knew that much. She used to have a cold heart that cared little about others and didn't let people disappearing from her life bother her. Now she was…heartbroken.

Was she actually in love with Logan? Was that it? Had being nice, changing her ways, and acting like a real human being, not the robot her mother wanted and trained her to be, royally fucked her up? Her phone chimed and her heart fluttered.

It was the sound she'd assigned to Logan.

How are you? His text read.

Frowning, she stabbed at the keyboard. *Fine.*

Good to hear.

Good to hear? Good to fucking hear? Her blood felt as if it had started to boil in her veins and her face went hot as anger flooded through her. Good to hear? He hadn't even bothered to call to actually hear her say it. He'd sent another text message.

She put her phone down to keep herself from typing something she might regret.

Words like 'go fuck yourself', 'don't bother', and 'I'm done with you' might come out. Words she'd said to Joe when she was angry with him, but not words she wanted to say to Logan. Alright, she did, she felt like saying them would release some of this hurt and anger, but would it accomplish anything?

The phone chimed again.

What's wrong? The message asked.

I miss you. I want to see you. It's been three weeks, Logan. Why are you avoiding me? Do you hate me now?

She typed the message out with a swipe of her fingers, fixed the words auto-correct decided were meant to be other words, then hit send. And waited.

I'll drop by later this evening.

The rage ebbed away, as did the hurt, forced out of her body by the happy pounding of her heart. He would be over. Tonight. Thank fuck.

Great, I'll be waiting.

And she would be, she decided. She ran into the bathroom after she cleared away the signs of the dinner she'd shared with Rosa, took a shower, and did her hair and makeup. Her hair was in lustrous golden curls down her back and her makeup perfectly highlighted her light gray eyes. They'd been the color of an angry rainstorm over the last few weeks, but now that Logan was coming over, their shade had lightened with her mood.

She went to her lingerie drawer and looked inside. She took out the black silk and lace garter belt she'd found at a boutique, a pair of lacy black stockings, and a black lace bra. To the lingerie, she added a white silk robe that skimmed around her mid-thigh and his favorite pair of black heels. She didn't need anything else, she decided, until she spotted the pendant on a fine gold chain that he'd sent her earlier in the week. A butterfly cast in gold with tiny diamonds accenting the wings.

She'd always loved butterflies and had thought the gift was wonderful, if unnecessary. But she'd wear it tonight. For him.

There were no moments lost on second-guessing herself or castigating herself for being his toy. She wanted to be with him, however that happened. She didn't know if she loved him, if she was capable of loving anyone, except Rosa of course, but she thought...maybe she did.

Memories of their time together flooded into her brain as she waited, another glass of wine in her hand. She wanted to relax before he got there, unwind some so that she wouldn't come off like some needy schoolgirl with her first boyfriend. By the time she finished the drink the sun had disappeared and she was nodding off to the soft music playing in the background.

It was after 10 pm, but he'd said later this evening. That could be any time at all. Just because he hadn't arrived yet didn't mean he'd bailed on her. Maybe she'd just have a little nap, she decided, as the alcohol in the wine tugged her into a peaceful sleep. She'd barely slept over the last week, even though she needed the rest to do her homework with any kind of ability. She'd turned in a few assignments with misspellings, but her instructors had let it pass.

When she woke up at 2 am, needing the bathroom, she knew he wasn't coming. She looked at her phone, disappointment bringing tears to her eyes. She cleaned her face, changed into a nightgown, and went to bed. Alone.

Why had he lied to her?

18

Logan

*H*e'd didn't hate her, and it hurt that Keily had even asked him that. He'd stayed away to protect her, to keep her from the abuse he might pile on her in the wake of his nightmares. The dream hadn't stopped plaguing him and that always turned him into an asshole. Not the physically abusive kind of asshole, but the kind that might say things he didn't want to say to her anymore. Nasty things that would break her.

He'd stayed away from her to protect her, to keep her from having to shoulder the burden of his misery. He was an exhausted mess and he didn't want to expose her to that. Sleepless nights, busy days, left him running on empty. Those weren't his best times.

He realized how long he'd avoided her when she asked him that question. It had been far too long and he wondered if some time with her might help him. He missed her too, whether he liked it or not.

Waking up every night with the smell of his own burning flesh in his nose, knowing it was only a memory and not real, but still smelling it, didn't make him the kind of person anyone should have to be around the next day. He knew that and knew Keily didn't deserve his current...state.

Maybe some time with her would calm him down long enough to sleep through the night?

He was about to leave the office, about to walk out the door with the keys in his hand, when his phone started going crazy with alerts and text messages. Then it started to ring too. "What the hell?"

He pulled the phone out of his trouser pocket and answered the phone.

"Logan? Logan have you heard yet?" Wally, his right-hand man in California, asked breathlessly on the other end of the line. He sounded erratic, shaken, and...scared.

"Heard what, Wally?" Logan stared at the elevator, but he didn't see it. He was focused solely on Wally's voice. Something was wrong.

"There was an earthquake. The whole building

has collapsed, Logan. I'm trapped inside with my assistant and the head of HR."

"Why aren't you on the phone with emergency services, Wally?" Logan demanded, but Wally interrupted his tirade.

"I have, they're outside now, trying to get to us. Logan, it's bad, really bad. I think, fuck, Logan, it's bad." Wally's voice broke up and Logan went into pro-mode.

"Listen, Wally, I'm on my way. I'm sure emergency services will get you out. Just hang tight man, okay? Let me get on a plane, and I bet you're out before I even land."

"I hope so, Logan. Melanie's leg is broken and she's pregnant." Wally answered, and Logan pictured the cute brunette that worked as Wally's personal assistant.

"You're all going to be okay, I swear it, man. One way or another, we'll get you out of there."

Logan had no idea how he'd keep that promise, but he got off the phone with that conviction in mind. He got on the first plane he could catch and sped out to California with nothing on his mind but his employees and their safety. His parents were out of range of the earthquake, so he knew they were fine. He got a call from his mom while he was getting off the plane in California, surprised to see her name on the screen. He told her he was fine too and that he was busy, so he kind of brushed her off, but she didn't take it personally, he knew. It was how they were.

He spent a week in California, trying to sift through rubble, paperwork, and insurance claims as the days blurred into one. As he'd assured Wally, he and everyone else in the building were evacuated without any loss of life. There were a lot of injuries, but he'd take that over death. The earthquake, bigger than any on record, had decimated buildings. The loss of life in the other buildings cast a somber air over the entire city, but it was the people that had lost their homes that concerned Logan the most. He paid for temporary shelters to be brought in, mini-mobile homes, and other more environmentally friendly temporary units, and donated money to charities left and right. He wasn't the only one working hard to keep his business while also trying to help the best way he could. He wanted to be there to help, in any way possible. This was his second home now, but it had a special place in his heart.

Logan knew he needed to send word to Keily somehow, but the first night passed with frantic phone calls, trips to the emergency room, and trying to find a place to house his employees who'd lost their own homes, as well as their place of employment. It was the middle of the night back there, so he told himself he'd call the next day. The next day was filled with just as many frantic trips across the city, calls to be made, and he knew he was needed more by his people than by Keily. She'd understand, he told himself. Surely she'd seen the news.

At the end of the week, he flew back to South Carolina, at last. He'd gone downtown one last time to go over the plan he'd formed with Wally to get started on clearing the disaster area that used to be his building. There were so many plans to be made that he knew the work wasn't done, but he had to get back to South Carolina for some meetings there he couldn't postpone.

After that meeting, he went back to his hotel and gathered his things. It was time to get back home. To Keily. He'd had a lot to think about over the last week, and he knew that all he wanted once he stepped off that plane was a shower, and to slip into bed with Keily. If she'd let him in her door. She hadn't texted him at all since that night when he hadn't gone to her house.

But fuck her if she didn't understand. Well, no, fuck him. He was the one that hadn't even sent her a message. Fuck, this might not be good, he thought as he got into his car and drove towards her place. Would she kick him out?

Logan let himself in with his key and noticed right away that the house was dark and quiet. It was after midnight, and her car was in its parking spot, so she must be asleep. Damn. What should he do?

He toed his black leather loafers off and removed his suit jacket. He was here now. Might as well see if he could make peace. After seeing all the death and destruction in California, he knew what he wanted from the future. If she'd let him, he'd use his body to show her what his mouth couldn't say. He headed for the bathroom, determined to wash the grime of the flight off his skin before he touched her. If that didn't wake her and have her demanding he get out, he'd take his chances.

He was naked by the time he made it to her room, unsure of how she'd react to his presence, but he knew the best way to deal with Keily was head-on. If she told him to fuck off, then that's what he'd do, but he had to try.

She was on her right side, the comforter pulled up to her chin, in the middle of the bed. It was freezing cold in the room, just the way she liked it when she slept, but it made goosebumps break out over his slightly damp skin. He'd be warm soon enough, if she didn't bash him over the head with a lamp or that baseball bat she kept at the left side of her bed.

He pulled the comforter up from her back and slid in to spoon her body into his.

"Keily. I'm here." He said as she stirred and then went stiff as a board. "It's okay, it's just me."

"Logan? What the fuck are you doing here? Go away." She asked sleepily, obviously angry, but too tired to argue. He didn't say anything, and he soon heard her snore softly.

"Keily? Wake up, honey." Okay, she'd told him to fuck off, but did she mean it? She was half-asleep, maybe she didn't mean it. He turned her to face him and her eyes popped open. She stared up at him, her face a blank mask that twisted into hurt anger as she gazed icily at him.

"Where the hell have you been?" She spit at him, but she didn't reach for anything so he decided he must be safe for now.

"The earthquake in California brought my building down. I had to go and take care of things there."

"Oh." She answered. "Well, when I wake up in the morning, if you're still here, I'll know it wasn't a dream. Otherwise, I'm going back to sleep."

It didn't really make sense, but she wasn't totally out of the Land of Nod yet.

"No, wake up, let me hold you. I've missed you."

"Hold me while I sleep, asshole." She mumbled and pushed her head into the space between his shoulder and neck. That meant he had to push his head up higher on the pillow, but if that was where she wanted to be, that's where she'd be.

For the longest time, he was content to just hold her, to feel her heartbeat as he cupped her left breast in his palm. It soothed him, and for a little while, he slept beside her. His dreams were peaceful, despite the nightmare that had plagued him and the week he'd had, the worries that kept him on edge. He was tired, too tired to fight off sleep as he found peace at last, for the first time since the nightmare began to plague him again.

It was dark, quiet sleep, the restorative kind that he hadn't had in a month now. The kind he always had with Keily in his arms. He wasn't even sure why he'd left her that first night, he thought as he woke up in the early hours of dawn, the sunrise still only a glow on the horizon.

He slid out of the bed, made sure she was still asleep, and made his way to the bathroom. A few minutes later he was in the kitchen brewing coffee in her French press and waiting to see what inspiration hit him. He had to go to the office later, but if he skipped his normal morning routine, he could wake her up and have her in his arms, wide awake and gasping in pleasure.

He drank the coffee, brushed his teeth with the toothbrush he'd left there, and went back to her bed. He slid in behind her once more and smiled when she moaned softly in delight. She might be asleep, but her body knew what it wanted.

Her nightgown, a white cotton slip really that came down to her knees, was hiked up over her hips. The feel of her smooth skin against his palm made his pulse pound as his mind whirled with other thoughts.

Logan held Keily in his arms and had to laugh at himself silently. Once upon a time, he'd have given anything to have a woman like Keily in his embrace. During his years at the university, he'd learned what it was like to want a woman. During his years after, he'd learned how to fuck women properly. He'd never wanted any of them the way he wanted her.

Still, it was nice to just hold her, which was something he'd never done with women, even in his younger days. He thought he'd never do such a thing, not until the first time he'd stayed over with Keily. Keily was amazingly sexy, even when she didn't try to be, but she was also a source of comfort. He hadn't realized just how much comfort he found in her until he was standing in the rubble of what had been the first building in his empire, wondering what to do next. He'd wanted to be with her then, but he couldn't be. He was here now, though, and if she'd let him, he'd make the most of it.

She was sleeping, unaware of the world around her, but she still managed to grab his attention. He inhaled the scent of her hair shampoo and her perfume filling his nose. That scent spawned need low in his groin, but it wasn't sexual need. It was a need to keep her close to him, to remind himself that she was really there, and this wasn't a nightmare he'd soon wake up from.

He was hard for her, ready for her, but that wasn't what he needed. Not yet. Keily whispered something in her sleep as he pressed into her, her body responding to the stimulus of his body behind her. The way she pressed back into him instinctively only made him harder, although he still didn't want to wake her. Not yet.

This was Keily at her most vulnerable, at a moment when she was…his. Nobody else got to see this side of her or touch her like this. Only him. He hadn't wanted to admit that was what he wanted for the longest time, to claim her as his own. But he couldn't get away from the idea of it, the need for her to always be there for him. For her to always be his.

It wasn't a good idea, he knew that, but that didn't stop his heart from wanting it, his brain demanding it. He'd never been in love before, didn't know if he was now, but he had to wonder. Did he love this woman?

He loved everything about her, the way she laughed, the way she smiled. The way she'd frown when she was unhappy about, or with, something. The determination she met life with was another thing he loved about her. She was still studying; he'd seen the books on her table, so he knew how determined she was. As if the determination to get the job he'd given her hadn't been enough to prove that, he thought ruefully.

She was also spirited, adventurous, curious, and full of life. What else could he ask for besides the beauty she came by naturally? She didn't even have to put makeup on, she was beautiful without it. She was everything he hadn't known he wanted in a woman and for once...he was good with that.

19

Logan

Keily's warmth seeped into him as he held her. She surprised him when she turned and pushed her left leg between his, her breath hot against his neck. Now might be the time.

With a gentle touch, he pushed a hand under her nightgown, up to her breast to lightly stroke a nipple. Her body moved against him, slowly, but enough to make him groan quietly. Her head moved as his fingers grasped the tip tighter, her eyes on his. She was awake now.

"Don't say anything just let me touch you." He whispered, wanting to keep the peace of the moment.

Her answer was to push her breast deeper into

his hand. He felt the warm glide of her left hand over his back, an answer to the question he hadn't asked. She wanted him, that's all that mattered.

He forgot about the last few weeks as he brought his lips to hers and lost himself in the world they created together.

Logan smiled against her lips when her hand moved up to cup his neck, to pull him closer to her. She couldn't get enough either.

He moved to tuck her under his body, ready to take her, to be in her, but wanting to remind himself of every inch of her at the same time. It had been too long since he'd touched her like this, tasted her, smelled her.

She wanted to touch him, it seemed. Her hands roved, stroking him, massaging in places, before her right hand slid down his abdomen to the very part that needed her most right now. He gasped as her fingers closed around him, teased him with soft, short strokes.

He wanted to growl at her to stop, to not make him come because it had been too long and he needed her desperately, but he held the words back. Instead, he thrust into her hand, let her have what she wanted, while he gritted his teeth to hold back.

He couldn't help a moan of appreciation when her tongue slid up to touch his throat, her lips a silky touch down his neck, before she sought out and found a nipple. Her tongue stroked the flat circle into a peak and he had to admit, he loved it when she did that. Fuck, he wanted to come, but he had to wait, had to make sure she got there first.

She sighed against his skin when he thrust into her hand a little harder, a little faster, urging her to get on with it or to stop. She was driving him crazy.

Her right hand moved, dug into the round flesh of his ass to drive him into her hand and his patience snapped. That simple touch broke his will as the other touches hadn't. He needed to calm down, he knew that, and instead of driving into her, he moved down her body, pushing the nightgown up over her breasts,

If she wanted to play, he'd play.

He moved down between her thighs, his lips almost grazing the damp skin that glistened in the early sunlight. But first, he cupped her breasts, eager to hear the sounds that only Keily could make for him. She gave a grunt of protest when he hovered over her skin, his hands only cupping the round flesh of breasts.

"Logan...." She breathed his name and that nearly snapped the will he'd only just regained control of. When she tilted her hips up to his face, he couldn't help but open his mouth, to taste her. He was powerless against that urge. His lips cupped at the soft skin of her labia while his tongue searched, and found, the part that ached for his touch the most.

Keily, still half asleep, twisted her hips in time with his tongue, lost in nothing but sensation. His fingers tightened on her nipples, driving her a little higher. Her hands came down, fluttered over his head, pressed his face deeper into her, before they flitted down to his shoulders. She held onto him there, danced on his tongue, her breath halting as she gave in to the pleasure he gave.

Logan listened, waited, tested the way he moved his tongue to make her breathing more erratic. It was then she was almost there, when she was just on the edge that her breaths would halt. She'd hold her breath and wait until the first wave of bliss passed over her before she'd gasp for air again.

He'd wanted to be inside of her desperately, but now? He wanted nothing more than to send her over the edge.

"Oh, Logan, please..." She begged, but he knew it was only words, she was just telling him she was almost there and needed him to keep going.

Her fingers dug into his shoulders until it was painful, but he took the pain, turned it into pleasure that only made his cock throb harder. Soon, he'd be inside of her, inside that delicious haven that got him off better than anything else ever had.

He'd been tempted to get himself off while he was apart from her, especially when his mind fucked with him and wouldn't let him stop thinking about her, but he knew it was a poor replacement for the real thing and hadn't bothered. That denial made him eager to get inside of her, to feel her surrounding him in luscious, wet heat.

But not yet.

He finally heard the sound, that little hitch before she held her breath, felt the way her hips pushed *down,* and knew not to let go. She lost all control, gasped his name, and made the most beautiful sounds he'd ever heard. This was what he'd wanted the most, that sound of pure bliss, and she rode that wave for ages. He didn't let go, not until she pushed against him, not until she whimpered in protest.

He'd wanted to slide right into her, but wanted to look up at her more, so he turned, pulled her over him, and groaned as she slid down onto his hard shaft, at last. Logan's brain turned off completely so that he could savor, for only a moment, that sweet moment when she took every last inch of him. It was an exquisite sensation that he didn't want to end, but sitting still would get them nowhere.

He opened his eyes to see her smiling down at him, just before she leaned over to kiss him, her hips moving in time with the guidance of his hands on them. She moaned into his mouth as she found just the right angle and let go of the kiss.

Something brushed at his nose as she moved away, her breasts at his chin. He pushed a necklace away, pushing the pendant behind her neck to keep it out of the way as she sought one more chance to experience heaven. Logan was too hungry for her to hold back too much, but he did his best. If he didn't last this time, he'd make it up to her. He always did.

Time stood still as she moved on him and he had to open his eyes at last, to look at her, to see just how gorgeous it was to watch her ride him. She was lost in sensation, he saw as he looked up at her face. There was concentration in the way her brows knitted together, lust in the way her tongue swiped at dry lips, and then pleasure as her jaw came forward when she found the right spot.

She was fucking delicious, everything he remembered she was, and she was his again. There was no distracting himself now, not after that glance at her face. It was a siren call he couldn't resist, and he thrust up into her with enough force to lift his hips from the bed. There were no complaints, only the clamp of her thighs against his hips to make sure she stayed on for the ride.

Logan glanced down at her breasts as she pushed herself up to gain some traction. She understood instinctively that he was past waiting, past holding back, and wanted to help him now. She brushed her hair behind her shoulders, thrusting out her breasts as she did so. Logan was the one that gasped this time.

She was...perfect.

She shook her head as he groaned, letting her head fall back as he fucked her just right, and the pendant fell back down her neck to nestle just at the very top of her breasts. It glinted for a moment, but Logan closed his eyes before he could make out the design. He didn't give a fuck what that necklace was, not when he was about to die if he didn't come soon.

His fingers dug into her hips, held her in place as she thrust harder, every inch slamming into her welcoming body, until he thought he'd leave bruises on her skin, but he knew she didn't care. She never complained about what happened when they had sex, as long as they both got off, that was all she cared about.

She'd had hers already, it was his turn now.

"Look at me, Logan, look at me while you fuck me." Her voice intruded into the darkness behind his eyelids and he did as she asked.

Light gray eyes stared down into his and she smiled. She liked it when he obeyed.

"That's it, watch me, look at me, know it's me that's getting you off." She'd become bolder since they went on vacation together, definitely more talkative in the bedroom, and he loved it.

"I'm watching you, Keily. I see you." He assured her.

Another gasp escaped him as he watched her, saw how dark her nipples were, such a contrast to the lightness of the rest of her, saw how her eyes devoured every sign of his pleasure, and nearly slipped away. Nearly. He held on, wanting to enjoy this for as long as he could.

Getting off was only half the fun. The getting there was just as fun and being inside Keily was a bliss all its own. There wasn't anywhere else he wanted to be and getting off would mean that his time in that precious place was over. For a little while, anyway.

"Don't you want to come, Logan?" She asked and he knew by the way she breathed that she was about to fly high again.

"I do, Keily, but I do love fucking you."

"I know." She purred as she fought to move her hips, still locked in his grasp.

"I don't hate you anymore." The words slipped out. He wanted to unsay them, but that was impossible. You could never unsay words already spoken, he'd learned that a long time ago and had tried to remember it all times, but he couldn't remember a damn thing that he should when he was inside of her.

"I don't know if that's true, Logan, but it's alright. You're here now and that's all I care about."

She responded, and there wasn't much else he could say to that.

He decided to shut up before he admitted something more, something he shouldn't, and concentrated on what he'd worked so hard for. Pure bliss.

Her nails raked down his chest as he felt the first slight twinge of what was to come. When she dug the hard tips in, he felt a pulse of pleasure that blew his mind and his balls.

His eyes flew open as that pulse came again. He groaned from somewhere deep in his chest and as pleasure coursed through straight up to his brain, his eyes caught on the pendant. He didn't really see it at first, all he could concentrate on was how he felt, the sound of Keily encouraging him, but then his brain settled a little.

Where did that come from? It took him a minute to remember he'd bought it accidentally. He'd wanted to get her the one next to it, but he'd been in a rush that day. Instead of going through the process of getting a refund, he'd let the sale go through at the online jeweler where he'd bought it.

A butterfly encrusted with tiny diamonds.

Butterfly.

Memories burst alive inside his mind, came back to haunt him as a smell in his nose.

That fucking necklace.

Why hadn't he just asked for a refund? Was it to taunt her? To remind himself in some kind of fucked up unconscious way that he shouldn't be with her?

He swiped at his nose and pushed her gently off of his hips to sit up on the edge of the bed. Shame, humiliation, pain coursed through him as the memories played out. Anger replaced the familiar emotions; her scent replaced the smell of charred flesh. The anger bloomed, became something strong that he couldn't ignore or swallow down.

That fucking butterfly necklace.

In an instant, everything changed. Seeing that necklace dangling around her neck brought rage instead of happiness.

The sounds of an 18-year-old young man screaming in agony filled his head, the sound of laughter, a shrill protest that was followed by a slap of flesh against flesh. The girl stopped screaming at the boys to stop, but the boys didn't stop. They used that stick to press the keychain, two inches around, deeper into the skin of his buttock. It was smooth now, the scar tissue barely noticeable, unless you saw it.

He'd taken pains to ensure she'd never seen it, that nobody ever did. If he'd gotten the butterfly placed on his ass as a drunken tattoo or even as a scarification that he'd wanted it wouldn't have mattered. But he hadn't asked to be attacked that night, he hadn't asked to be a part of those boys' sick pleasure at his screams.

And Keily now had a butterfly he'd given her hanging around her neck.

Fuck.

He had to leave, he had to get out of there.

He remembered now why this was all a bad idea, why he shouldn't have hired a woman like her in the first place.

She wasn't the right one for him, he couldn't love a woman like her, even if she was all but perfect. He was still too broken to ever love anyone properly. He might never be able to love a woman, or anyone else properly.

Keily was completely unaware of what was going on inside Logan's head. She had rolled to face away from him and hadn't spoken yet. She might even be asleep again. He didn't know and right now it didn't matter. He had to leave her place, not come back, that was the only way any of this would end.

He hadn't had the nightmares for years, but they'd started again. The only way to banish the hell was to go back to the predictable, empty, but profitable life he'd lived before. And leave her.

20

Keily

"*Y*ou're leaving?" She rolled over as she felt him get up from the bed.

"I am, yes." He answered softly, searching around for his clothes.

"Logan? Why are you leaving?" But her eyes had fallen on the scar and she stared at it. Was that a...butterfly?

Memories flared to life, memories she'd banished from her mind. A drunken night at the pond, the screams of a helpless boy, her own screams at Joe to stop and let the boy go. She'd been unhappy when they pulled the guy out of the woods, she'd been angry when Joe had ripped her favorite keychain from her hands, and terrified when Joe ordered his buddies to hold the guy down.

When she protested louder, shrieked at Joe to stop, he'd slapped her. It hadn't been the first time he'd slapped her, only the first time he'd done it in front of others. He'd hissed at her that she'd be next if she didn't pipe down, but she'd still protested. Only, not as loud as before.

She couldn't stop the memory of that gangly boy's screams that night, or the smell as Joe had branded the guy with her keychain. She'd suppressed that memory, hid it from herself as best as she could. But that boy's name hadn't been Logan. He hadn't looked like Logan either.

He'd been goofy, a nerd that she'd barely taken notice of throughout high school. Now, she couldn't forget his face. But that wasn't Logan's face. Was it?

Joe and his buddies hadn't just been drunk that night. They'd snorted one too many lines of coke and were out of their minds. The way Joe had growled at her, hissed at her that she'd be next if she didn't shut up, had truly frightened her. Joe was a prick on good days, on coke he was another beast entirely. One she didn't want to poke too much.

Her cries of protest had died down and they'd eventually let the kid go. He hadn't been crying, he'd been screaming. Keily thought it must be the pain, but she knew it was humiliation too. She'd looked away as Joe dragged her to his car, wondering how she was going to get into her house without her key.

And she'd lived with that memory locked away ever since.

Eugene.

That had been the boy's name. Eugene Baumgarten. Not Logan Sinclair.

But as he pulled his pants over his ass and turned around to put his shirt on, Keily saw it. The anger in his eyes, the features that had morphed from a boy's features to a man's.

"Eugene?" Even as she questioned him, she knew it couldn't be. He'd have said something, wouldn't he? Shock washed over her as Logan smirked.

"Noticed that finally, have you?" He put his shirt on, a cold smirk on his face. "I guess that's about all the explanation you need then. Oh, by the way, we're done, Keily. Have a nice life. I won't be in it anymore."

"What? Logan, wait." She rushed from the bed, not caring that she was a mess. She needed to stop him as he walked out of the bedroom.

"No, Keily. That's it. We're done." He came to a sudden halt in her hallway and turned to face her. "I'll let you keep the apartment and the car, but otherwise? We're done. Now please, don't make this about you and let me go."

"But…" She stared up at him. The man who'd gazed up at her with complete adoration in his eyes only a few minutes ago now stared down at her with cold…emptiness. She'd been a part of the reason he was like that. Whether she'd tried to stop it or not, she hadn't, and she'd lived with the man that had done it. She'd married him, to make it even worse.

There was nothing she could say to take it back. To make it better. She couldn't make him stay. Not after what they'd done to him.

Her mouth closed and he turned away. She heard his footsteps as he walked away, heard the sound of the door closing. It was over.

She went back to her bed, crawled in, and pulled the covers over her head. Tears streamed down her face and sobs broke the silence, but she wasn't aware of it.

Emptiness, loss consumed her for hours. Her phone buzzed, she remembered for a moment that she was supposed to meet Rosa for breakfast but didn't care. Logan was gone and gone for good.

Her heart was truly broken now. She'd spent the last few weeks almost positive it was over. Then, when he hadn't shown up last week as he'd promised, she'd been even more certain. She'd learned about the earthquake, saw the damage on her television screen, and had breathed a sigh of relief. It had struck that night he didn't show up. He must have flown out to get there immediately.

Logan's employees were incredibly important to him and she'd read that his was one of the buildings that collapsed. She'd excused his absence, his lack of communication and when he slid into her bed late last night, she'd been too glad that he was there to be angry. Instead of telling him to get out she simply accepted his presence with a sigh of happiness.

He was back, all would be well. When he'd woken her up to the sweetest touch she'd ever known, she'd felt hope spring to life. They could get past whatever had kept him away. They could make this work. They could be together, have a future.

If she'd known that was the last time that she'd ever touch him she'd have spent more time memorizing his body, she'd have made it last a little longer. She hadn't known, though. She never suspected who he was, never even wondered about how he could be from King's Hill, but she had no idea who he was.

When he first arrived, she hadn't known that he was from the area, but she'd gleaned that information from things he said. It just never occurred to her to ask him why she didn't recognize him. Why she didn't know his name.

She still didn't know where he got the name

Logan Sinclair from but knew it must be his legal name now because it was the one he signed on all his legal documents. He must have had it changed, well, obviously he had, she thought as she sat up and swiped at her face with the towel that had been wrapped around her hair when she fell asleep the night before.

He was that poor boy that Joe had assaulted. The one she'd walked away from without a backward glance. Every now and then the memory would try to surface but as the years passed, she'd managed to bury it deeper and deeper. Joe had replaced it with more bad memories, she'd learned to stand up to him over time, and eventually, she'd walked away from him.

Joe never mentioned that night, or Eugene, and Keily wondered now if Joe even remembered it. Probably not. He'd dropped her at home and gone out to raise more hell with his buddies. He probably didn't remember anything about that night at all.

Was that why Logan came back? To get revenge on Joe? To make him pay for what he'd done? There was no better revenge than success, or so she'd heard one too many times. Logan, Eugene, had certainly become a success. He'd brought life back to a town that had given him nothing but pain and humiliation. Because it wasn't just that night that had brought misery to that kid.

Joe and his friends had tormented him for as long as Keily could remember. Even she'd said snide things to him when Joe was around, just to get a smile from the jerk. To feed his already massive ego. Not that hers hadn't been huge as well, she'd been no angel when it came to that.

Had Logan known who she was from the start? He had to, everyone knew her name back then, knew who she was. Was that why he'd hired her without too many questions? Why he'd tormented her until she broke down and quit?

Yeah, he'd wanted to sleep with her, that was mutual, but he'd been an absolute jerk to her, and she'd hung on until she couldn't take any more. Then she'd become his mistress.

Humiliation washed over her as she thought over the last few months. He must have known who she was all along, then. This must have been part of his plan.

Had she just been some revenge fuck? A way for Logan, Eugene, to get back at Joe and his friends? She must have been. That's why he'd walked out the door, after all, wasn't it?

He had such a cold look on his face when he left that she knew, deep down, that he wasn't coming back. That he'd taken what he wanted, and he was done with her now. Just like every other fucker in her life.

Rosa had been right, after all. Logan hadn't loved her at all. He'd only used her.

That was, oddly, something she could understand. She was used to that. What she couldn't understand was how he'd looked at her with so much adoration as he'd fucked her in the early morning light, then turned so cold after.

The necklace tugged at her skin as she rolled over in the bed and she tugged it to free it from where it was sticking to her skin.

Then she remembered what it was. A butterfly.

She took the necklace off and held it in her hand. A butterfly, not much different from that keychain. How could she not have seen the hint he'd given her? It was right here, all this time. He'd told her exactly who he was, but she'd been too self-involved, still, to let herself put the two together. She just assumed he'd noticed how much she liked butterflies, even after what Joe had done with her keychain.

When you suppress a memory, it's possible to not have an aversion to reminders of what had happened. Or so she'd heard, learned, as the years passed her by. It had been seven years and she hadn't allowed the memory to do anything but nudge the surface since. She'd walked away, not looked back, and done what was expected of her. As she always did.

And he'd used that against her.

He'd used her own need to actually be loved for once in her life against her. Then he'd thrown her away like a toy he was tired of playing with. That hurt, it really did. But not as much as knowing she'd never touch him again. That brought to life an ache unlike anything she'd ever experienced before. Worrying that she'd never get a chance to touch him again wasn't nearly as bad as *knowing* she wouldn't.

How was she supposed to recover from this? Could she recover from it? Even her sadness that Violet wouldn't return her calls didn't hurt as much as this loss did. Maybe that was still selfish of her, but she'd always had a fragile relationship with her sister. She'd pinned unspoken hopes on Logan, she'd dared to dream of a future with him. She'd even wondered about more than that. Wanted more than that.

Sniffling, she put the necklace on her nightstand, but couldn't take her eyes off of it. How could she decorate her life with those things after what Joe had done? Had Logan looked at every one of her pictures, figurines, and felt a stab of pain? Had he seen it as insensitivity, carelessness, cruelty on her part?

She hadn't meant them that way. She saw butterflies as a representation of herself. Flighty things that went where their biology told them to go, but with short lifespans. Easily damaged, yet vital to the earth in so many ways. The insects were a sign of beauty and hope to her and that's how she'd always seen them. Even after that night. Despite that night.

And now she could barely look at the necklace without shame filling her. She'd had no clue about who he really was. And now he was gone.

There were no words she could say to defend what she'd done, or hadn't done, that night. She could have called the police, reported it. She could have approached him at their graduation and asked if he was okay, offered to help him press charges. Instead, she'd gone home, gone to bed, and got up to preen with her friends the next day as if nothing had happened at all.

She'd been just as culpable as they had been when she didn't go to the police. She could have checked on him, at the very least. But she'd already been in the process of letting it all go, of pushing the memory away from her. What Joe and his friends had done had been deplorable. It wasn't a boyish prank; she'd seen the evidence of just how awful that night had been in the vivid scar on his ass. It had been a brutal assault that would have made the papers if it had been done to a woman. If he'd reported it.

It must have pained him for a long time and seeing the mark must have been a reminder of that every time he saw it. Cold certainty filled her the more she thought about it. He'd said they were done, and she had no doubt of that at all. He wouldn't have said it if he didn't mean it.

She couldn't blame him, either. She'd allowed something beyond awful to happen to him, and then she'd kept quiet. It didn't matter if she'd changed, become a better person than she was even a year ago. She was still that girl that kept her mouth shut and had then married a man so brutal he'd marked another man, assaulted him in a most degrading way. A way that had marked that other man for life.

There was no way she could expect forgiveness for that. There was no way she could ask him to accept that she wasn't that same girl who'd left him screaming by a fire, in utter agony both physically and mentally. There was no coming back from that.

It was done, and she knew it. For the first time in her life, she couldn't stop the tears, couldn't stop the pain, and knew, deep down, that she deserved every second of it. Even if he'd come back to town with humiliating her in mind, of getting back at Joe, she couldn't blame him for that either. Joe and his friends had tried to destroy Logan that night. Instead, he'd become better than all of them. She was happy about that, that he'd become such a success, but he deserved love.

Because of her and Joe, she doubted that would ever happen. It didn't help that she still wanted to be the one that gave him the love he needed. That was impossible now, and she knew it. There was nothing she could do to make it right and her life with him was over. Maybe, she thought, maybe that was exactly what she deserved.

But was it really? Rosa would tell her it wasn't, but Keily thought that a lonely, heartbroken life might be exactly what she deserved. Women like her didn't deserve happiness and never would.

Thank you for reading Twisted Love.
Follow Keily and Logon in Twisted Fate now.

The queen could do no wrong.
But it doesn't mean she did no harm.

Like most bullies, Keily had no idea she was one.
Then just as she was falling hard for Logan...
She realized it was all a plot.

A plot designed especially for her.

For being the queen of nasty.
For being the key to a dreadful crime committed
years ago.

That's right. Karma is a bitch.
There's no denying that she deserved it.

The question is, when will this punishment end?
Will she ever be forgiven?
Was it only ever revenge?
Or were some of those feelings real?

Get book 3, Twisted Fate now.
Or save 30% when you buy the next ebook directly
from my website.
https://payhip.com/b/qU90u
Use exclusive discount code:
BACK4-TF

SUMMER COOPER

DISCOVER THE WILD GIRL IN YOU

*B*esides her love of chocolate, dogs and music... reading and writing is Summer's number one route to escape from crazy friends, family and the in-laws!

She found her own happily ever after with a martial arts fighter who also happens to be an adorable IT geek! Now, she loves to write about hot alpha males that come with a pretty face and covered in tough-as-nails muscle... who are secretly looking for their true soul mate (shhh...)!

Visit her website at
www.summercooper.com

Follow her on
Facebook | Instagram
Goodreads | Bookbub | TikTok

Get in touch at
hello@summercooper.com